Kauai Kisses

Shelby Maerker

Kauai Kisses

Olympia Publishers
London

www.olympiapublishers.com
OLYMPIA PAPERBACK EDITION

A CIP catalogue record for this title is
available from the British Library.

ISBN: 978-1-80439-906-4

First Published in 2024

Olympia Publishers
Tallis House
2 Tallis Street
London
EC4Y 0AB

Printed in Great Britain

Dedication

This book is dedicated to all of the Zoeys in the world.

Acknowledgments

Thank you to Ty and Valkyrie for supporting me through this journey. Thank you to my dad for raising me to be a strong, independent woman. Thank you to my aunt and uncle, the ones who took me to Hawai'i for the first time, igniting my passion for the islands. To Rachel and John David, you've always been my brother and sister. I want to thank my best friend, O'Brien, and my Olive Garden family.

I must send a huge *mahalo* to the Hawaiian Islands. Without experiencing your beauty and culture, there would be no book.

Chapter 1

My name is Zoey Martin. My birthday is August 6, 2000. I have green eyes, and my nose is somewhat crooked from a fall I took down the stairs, when I was six. I had two wonderful parents, who experienced everything life has to offer. My mom was a nurse in the local hospital, but in her free time she loved to paint, drink tea, and tend to her rose bushes that made up the perimeter of our backyard. My dad was your average dad, in the midst of growing a beer belly, always prepared with a cheesy dad joke. He worked for an IT company in our hometown of Grand Haven, Michigan. My parents were honest, kind people who found faith in humanity. They found happiness in hiking through the forests and disappearing on spontaneous road trips. They visited the Great Wall of China, Area 51, and snorkeled in the great barrier reefs of Australia.

But not me. I haven't even traveled outside of the state of Michigan. My parents would beg me to come on their grand adventures, but I would always be so focused on my studies and perfecting my grades. I had dreams of becoming a doctor, to be able to provide a stable lifestyle for myself. It was my goal to be valedictorian of my high school and then to be accepted into an Ivy League college. My school of preference being Harvard. I stayed home and studied, volunteered at the local animal shelter, worked part-time at the Goodwill store, ran the school yearbook club and tutored math students in the middle school. I did everything I could to build an amazing resume that would benefit me when it was time to apply for college. *But now?* If I could go back and throw those textbooks in the trash, I would. If I could get back all of the community service hours that I wasted my weekends on, I would. If I could get on a plane and fly to an unexplored city with my parents, I would. *But now?* They're dead and I can't.

One night, my parents were in Montana and decided to take a late-night drive through the mountains. They got hit by a truck driver, who had fallen asleep behind the wheel, both dying before they even made it to the hospital. They took my life with them that night. I stopped participating in my extracurricular activities, my grades suffered, I barely graduated, and I definitely was not valedictorian. I didn't bother applying to college. Since I was fifteen at the time, I was forced to move in with my aunt, uncle, and two cousins. They are rich, snobby people who care nothing about anyone but themselves. It seemed to be such a burden for them to have to take me in. I don't even think they shed a tear at my mom and dad's funeral.

I got a job at the local diner to take care of myself, making adequate money. Nowhere near as much as my uncle though. Uncle Dan is a computer software engineer. My cousins, Denise and Samson, have been fed from golden spoons their entire lives by my aunt who was a proud stay-at-home mother. They do not know the true value of a dollar. Samson is attending Brown University to become an optometrist, not having to pay for any part of it himself. My aunt and uncle are very proud of him. Denise got a new Porsche for her eighteenth birthday, complaining that the color wasn't red like she had requested. Do you know what they got me for my birthday? Squat. Nada. Zilch. They didn't even wish me happy birthday. The last birthday when I received a present was when I had turned fifteen and my dad passed down his old Bronco to me, so that I could start learning how to drive. It was my favorite birthday, but also my last. My parents died three weeks later.

My aunt announced at breakfast this morning, that to celebrate her and my uncle's twentieth anniversary, we were all going to Hawaii. Kauai to be specific. Even me. Apparently, I can't be trusted in their house alone or maybe they think that I will call children services on them while they're gone. I have been told to stay out of their way and that they weren't paying for my part aside from the plane ticket. Hopefully, I will be able to relax quietly on the beach with a book, avoiding all of the drama I am sure will follow.

Chapter 2

I don't have many possessions. I have my dad's old rucksack that he used to take on all of his trips. He always said that it was his good luck charm. He left it in the hotel room the night they died. I don't exactly believe in luck but I can't help but to wonder, if maybe they would have survived if they had had the bag with them. I carry it everywhere. Inside it, I keep all of the things that are important to me; my mother's necklace of my birthstone, my father's copy of 'The Outsiders' that he liked to read to me at bedtime when I was little, a hairbrush, a coconut ChapStick, and a small family photo album with pictures of Mom, Dad, and myself. It helps to keep them close.

"We are leaving in five minutes! You better be ready, Zoey!" I hear Aunt Susan yell up the stairs angrily. I toss my anxiety medication into my bag and then rush out to the car. I am waiting there when everyone else walks out. I could hear my aunt whisper to my uncle that maybe I wouldn't be ready and that they could leave without me. I can't help but smirk when she sees me leaning against the car, ready to go, before my given five minutes are up.

"Oh, I guess you're here," Aunt Susan snarls at me.

"Yep, right on time like you asked," I respond, feigning submission.

We all climb in and begin the uncomfortable ride to the airport. When we get there, Denise pushes past me, knocking me out of the car, so that she can get in line first, to get her bags checked, as if that will get her to Hawaii faster. I hide my laugh as the airport employee weighing her bag tells her that it is twenty-eight pounds overweight and that she will have to pay a $75 fee. She stomps her foot as my uncle breaks out his credit card. Once we get all of our bags checked, we head to the gate to sit and wait. Aunt Susan insisted on us being there three hours early so now we have time to kill.

I get comfortable in my plastic, well-worn chair and pull out my dad's book. I couldn't tell you how many times I have read it. It makes me feel close to him. He used to tell everyone that when I was four, I believed Ponyboy was actually a half-pony half-boy hybrid and that I was very concerned about a pony eating bologna sandwiches. I wish I could hear him tell that story one more time. Before long, they were calling our group to board the plane just as I was getting to the part where Johnny and Ponyboy catch the train to Windrixville.

"I get the window seat, bitch," Denise says, pushing her way through to our aisle of seats.

"You can have it. I really don't care," I reply.

Denise takes the window seat. Samson sits in the middle. And I get the lovely aisle seat. Samson reads his medical journals all the while I am getting beat in the face with purses and elbows. Aunt Susan and Uncle Dan are in first class. I guess they wanted to be away from us for a while.

My legs are shaking—this is my first flight. I slip one of my anxiety pills into my mouth and swallow it with the 7-UP the flight attendant provided to help with my nausea. I lean my head back in my chair trying to relax when my seat gets a strong kick from an obnoxious six-year-old behind me. I turn to look at him only to see his mother completely ignoring her kid. This one I let go. He is just a kid after all. I face forward then *bam*! He does it again. *Bam! Bam! Bam!* I've had it. I turn around to address his mother as politely as possible.

"Excuse me, ma'am? Your son is kicking my chair. Could you ask him to stop, please?"

She stops her conversation to roll her eyes at me and says hotly, "He's having fun."

"Yes, I understand, but I'm not. It's uncomfortable. Can you please make him stop?"

"No," she states flatly. She returns to her conversation as if I were not there.

The kid continues kicking my chair, so the next time I see the flight attendant, I tell her about the kid behind me. She glares at the mother and mean-mugs the kid.

"I'll take care of you, honey. Grab your things and follow me."

I am confused, but I do as she says. *Who am I to question a flight attendant?* She walks to the front of the plane up to first class.

"I'm sorry. Am I being thrown off this flight?" I ask because I have no other explanation as to why she would bring me this far up the plane.

She laughs. "No silly. I am giving you one of the open seats in first class. All the drinks and meals are free up here, so feel free to take full advantage."

"Wow. That's so nice of you. Thank you so much. I really appreciate it."

"And I appreciate the gift bag of candy you gave me. You see us flight attendants as humans, not servants, and that kindness deserves to be rewarded."

I am in a seat in first class. It's the single seat behind all of the rest so Aunt Susan and Uncle Dan do not know I am up here.

Yet. Until the shrill squeals of Denise fill the entire plane. She is upset that I got a first-class seat and she didn't. Aunt Susan and Uncle Dan look back at me with a huff and tell me I should give Denise my seat. The flight attendant overhears this and steps in.

"I'm sorry. She can't give up her seat. I assigned that one specifically for her. If you would like, for a $200 upgrade fee we can move the other lady up here." Uncle Dan pulls out his credit card with a heavy sigh. Denise comes prancing up with a "Thanks, Daddy!" The flight attendant winks at me and then puts Denise in the open chair right next to Uncle Dan. Karma is a bitch.

Chapter 3

Take off wasn't as bad as I had expected. For the most part, the flight was pretty smooth and we encountered very little turbulence. I had several meals dropped off at my seat, including lots of cookies. Denise glared at me the whole time while I basked in my reward. The attention is never on me, so this is new, and if I am being honest, kind of a nice feeling. As we deplaned in Dallas, the flight attendant hugged me and told me to continue to be a nice human being. I smiled at her while my family rolled their eyes at the sentiment. We had an hour-and-a-half layover in Texas, in which the rest of my family had to stop at a restaurant so that Samson could get a bite to eat. He refused to eat anything from economy. I was too full from all of my snacks. Our plane to Kauai was delayed twenty minutes, so we all sat by the gate waiting to board.

The flight from Dallas to Kauai is a different story. It is a smaller plane, and we hit several patches of turbulence. I put my earbuds in and try to focus on the movie playing on the screen in front of me. Eight hours and four movies later, we finally arrive in Kauai. I am jittery, waiting to get off this plane. It takes forty-five minutes to deplane, and then we have to go find our luggage. Someone broke the lock on Denise's bag and sifted through her clothes.

Once we get out of the airport, we have to check in at the rental car kiosk, which was just outside the building. As we wait for the car to be brought up I finally take a look around at my surroundings. I can see the sand of the beach, palm trees swaying in the wind. The air smells so crisp and fresh. You can smell the earthy sea salt in the breeze. Nothing like the factory fumes back in Michigan. A nice silver Volvo drives up and it is nothing short of what I expected. Strong, rich, tourist vibes going on here. We pile in, with me of course getting stuck in the middle of Samson and Denise in the backseat. The drive to the rental house only takes about ten minutes.

Uncle Dan has rented us a beach house on a hill with a wide view of the ocean. It has four bedrooms, three baths, and a spacious, open kitchen with glass windows expanding from floor to ceiling. We have the most amazing view of the ocean which is probably just a few minutes' walk. I can only imagine what it would be like to live here and wake up to this every day. I am getting my own room in this beautiful beach house and am super excited. I wait for the others to choose their rooms first, knowing what would happen if I didn't. Aunt Susan and Uncle Dan take the master suite, which has its own bathroom and outdoor shower. Denise takes the second largest room. To my surprise, Samson takes one of the smaller rooms. Which leaves a small bedroom with a private bathroom on the opposite end of the house.

"Sam, are you sure you don't want this room? It has its own shower and toilet," I politely ask, seems only fair he should take it since his parents are the ones paying for it.

"No, that's all right. I don't feel like sleeping so close to where I pee. Do you know how much bacteria splashes out of the toilet bowl with each flush?"

I can't believe it. I can set all of my shower supplies and make-up out without having to put them away as soon as I am done. That's my routine back home. I'm not allowed to keep any

17

of my stuff out in the open because as I have been reminded time and time again 'it is not my house.'

I walk into my room and it feels like I belong here. The walls are painted a pale pink with a door leading outside into the garden. The entire room smells of flowers and there is a purple plumeria on my pillow. When I walk into the bathroom, I find little bottles of naturally made Hawaiian shampoo, lotion, and conditioner, and I instantly decide that is what I am going to use instead of my cheap ass Suave. The toilet paper has a flower rolled into it, which is so fancy to me. I never knew the privileges of being rich included toilet paper flowers. It seems excessive, but I'll indulge in it for a change.

I walk back into the main living area, where Samson is on the couch, with three different medical books open in front of him on the coffee table. His attention is deep into whatever is on his cell phone though. My aunt and uncle are smiling in the kitchen, and I assume that by Denise's absence, she is putting away all of her beauty products in her bathroom. *Me?* I am a simple foundation, eyeliner, mascara type of girl. *But Denise?* Oh no. She has all the powders, glitters, creams, and lip glosses that you could buy in an Ulta store. Aunt Susan yells for Denise asking what she feels like for dinner. No answer. So, they direct the question toward Samson.

"Pizza," Samson responds simply.

I look at him in amazement. "We are in Hawaii and you want pizza?"

He rolls his eyes at me. "Yes, pizza allows me to stay here and continue my studies while also consuming nutrients."

I roll my eyes and walk into the kitchen.

Uncle Dan addresses me, "What do you feel like?"

I never get a say in dinner choices. Even Aunt Susan looks

at him funny.

"Well, that seafood place we passed while driving here smelled really good," I respond.

"That's what I was thinking myself." He smiles.

Aunt Susan looks like she was about to have a fit. Denise walks out and Uncle Dan tells her we are eating at the seafood place down the street.

"I guess, but they better have steak," she huffs.

To my disappointment, we load back into the car. It's only a fifteen-minute walk but no one else wants to go on foot. I am crammed into the middle seat again, as we head to the restaurant.

The restaurant is gorgeous. The place is named The Lobster Hole with a huge lobster shell above the sign. It has an elegant fishing theme to it; the decorations include fishing nets draped across the white and blue walls with bobbers hanging on. There is a ship steering wheel set up as the host stand, and if you walk to the opposite side, you could walk out onto the beach. All of the doors were spread open letting the cool summer breeze drift in off of the water. My guess is that the doors only close during off hours and possibly storms. My uncle asks the host for a table for five outside. The weather here lifts my spirits. As I start looking through the menu, I realize this place is pretty ritzy. The menu ranges from lobster tail to crab cakes, mahi-mahi to eel, they even have a steak that would hopefully satisfy Denise. It is quite pricey with the cheapest option being an appetizer of four crab cakes that cost $22. I did not want to jump off the plane spending large amount of money but I figure this one dinner wouldn't hurt so I splurge on myself and order the mahi-mahi salad that costs $31. It's a good thing that I have been saving my money from working at the diner. My heart races. I haven't been this excited in years. I am trying not to let on to how much I am enjoying this.

Dinner comes and, of course, Denise has a problem with her steak so she sends it back, twice, frustrating our server. My mahi-mahi is decadent. Seared perfectly in a lemon garlic sauce. I savor every bite. Samson ordered the salmon which looks delicious as well. The server came back around with one check and I asked her if she could split mine off as I was paying for myself. She quickly took care of it and returned with two bills. Mine being $33.40 due to tax. I gave her a $50 and told her to keep the change. She smiled and looked truly thankful to receive a decent tip. My family, however, after getting the steak taken off the bill, spent $157 and left a ten percent tip. It amazes me how the rich can have so much money but are too cheap to tip their service providers. Everyone wants to go back to the house afterward, but I don't feel the same. I want to venture out to the beach, maybe get my feet wet. I ask if that would be all right and my aunt replies, "As long as, you're back in ten days when the plane takes off." That was a bit harsh. I can see my presence here is highly unwanted.

Chapter 4

I escape to the beach from the side entrance of the restaurant, taking my shoes off to squish my toes through the warm sand. I walk into the surf letting the water splash against my legs. As I walk, I take in the landscape around me. The smell of sea salt in the mist, the greenness of the trees and mountainside, and the nude skin color of the sand. My senses are on fire—burning in all of these new exposures. I pass kids splashing in the waves, moms smothering their babies in sunscreen, a couple being affectionate against a tree, kissing, and whispering to themselves. I walk past a rowdy bunch of guys kicking a soccer ball around in the sand. All of them shirtless. Each one is muscular with toned abs and bulky arms. There is one in particular that really catches my eye. He's tall with black tribal tattoos strewn across his skin. His hair is short, sun-kissed brown. And his skin, it's as if a Hawaiian God chiseled him from the volcano that formed the island. He is golden bronze and shimmering in droplets of sweat. It's like staring into a fire.

We just made eye contact. Shit! He caught me gawking at him. I give a small smile and look away, pretending like I wasn't just drooling at the sight of him. I keep walking until I wind up in a parking lot that is designated for this beach. The sun is starting to set, but I still have an hour or so before it's gone. Walking into the parking lot, I stop dead in my tracks. Right in front of me is the car of my deepest dreams. A neon orange Jeep Wrangler with a soft top rolled back and surfboard on top of the roll bars. This is my dream vehicle. I pictured mine a teal blue color but this orange is doing something for me. I didn't realize how close I had gotten to it, until I was looking inside, admiring the matching orange seat covers, and a collection of rubber ducks on the dash.

Someone behind me clears their throat. Shit! I probably look like a creep right now.

"You're not trying to steal my *yota*, right?" a smooth male voice asks behind me.

I literally want to crawl into a hole and die. I turn around, surprised to see the guy from the beach.

"*Uh* no, Sorry! I was just admiring. I've always dreamed of owning a Jeep."

"No worries." He moves around to throw his soccer ball in the back.

I take that as my cue to disappear. I start walking back the way I came but I stop when he speaks again.

"You're the chick that was checking me out on the beach a while ago, aren't you?"

I freeze, like a deer in headlights, when he calls me out. I turn around, playing cool.

"Nope, wasn't me."

"Yes, it was. You were walking, looking lost, until you saw me."

"I don't know what you're talking about, but I wasn't intentionally looking at you."

"It's cool if you were." He winks at me.

I smile. "I've got to go," I say, turning back around to leave this immensely awkward situation.

"See you around, *maka nani*."

I am too confused and embarrassed to ask what he just called me, an insult I assume. I jog a bit to get away from the parking lot. I figure I should head back to the beach house before it gets dark and I get completely lost. I slip my flip-flops back on and begin the mile trek back to the house. I could do this every day. Walk to the beach. Eat delicious fish. Watch hot guys play soccer.

Chapter 5

I wake up feeling refreshed, I slept in and it's almost eight-thirty a.m. I lie in bed for twenty more minutes scrolling through the news updates on my phone. This is nice to just lie around and relax but I know I need to get up. I stretch, walking into my bathroom to brush my teeth. It's kind of humid today, must be a pop-up storm moving in. I decide to rinse off in the shower and then style my hair with some gel. I dress in a pair of blue jean Bermuda shorts and a camo tank top. Even I've got to hand it to myself, I look good today. I feel more confident, like my old self. I apply a light coat of makeup, knowing I will sweat it off before lunch. Walking into the kitchen, I am met with my family in a whirlwind of cereal bowls and bagels. I grab a bagel and the cream cheese out of the fridge and jump into a seat at the kitchen island.

"Hurry up. We have to leave in fifteen minutes," my aunt barks at me.

Confused, I ask back, "Where are you going?"

My aunt storms away with a huff so Samson answers while finishing his cereal.

"We have a reservation for an ATV tour. The kind where you see the filming locations of *Jurassic Park* and *Indiana Jones*."

Oh. That sounds awesome. I guess I'll be left alone today while they go do that.

"Why is she so upset?" I ask Sam, motioning to my aunt.

"Because Dad told her that you are coming with us."

What? I'm coming too? I never get invited to do any sort of activity with them.

"Seriously?" I try to hide my excitement.

"Yep," he says, clearly not caring.

"Come on, everyone, let's get going." Uncle Dan walks through the kitchen heading out to the garage. My aunt huffing behind him and Denise skipping like the little princess she is. She is wearing a hot pink, string, bikini top with a white cover thing over it, and a pair of white, ripped short-shorts. I've never been on an ATV ride, but I'm pretty sure that's not the appropriate attire. I set my dirty plate in the sink, taking my uneaten bagel in the car with me.

We pull into a muddy driveway leading to a log cabin in the middle of a large piece of protected land. 'Piku Ranch' was handwritten in white on an old wooden sign made out of driftwood. A group of tourists stand in a grassy area waiting for their tour to begin. That's the same group we are to be a part of. Once we get parked, we go stand with all of the others. There is a short man in a bright, green shirt walking around checking people in. There are twelve blue and green ATVs ready to drive through the rough terrain, each only containing four helmets. I wonder where I'll be riding. The man in the green shirt walks over to us.

"*Aloha ohana.* What's the name?"

"Martin," my uncle responds.

"Martin. Got it. Reservation for four riders?" He eyes us, counting five.

"No, it's supposed to be for five." My uncle seems confused. He glances at my aunt who takes a sudden interest in a nearby tree.

"I'm sorry, sir, but the reservation that was made is only for four."

Uncle Dan looks at Aunt Susan. "Did you make the reservation for five like I asked?

"Well, I didn't think you were being serious. She shouldn't even be here. She's not part of our family. Can she just ride in the back or something? Maybe she can suck it in and squeeze between Samson and Denise." I look at her in shock. *Did she just call me fat?*

As my uncle opens his mouth to respond, and the man—his shirt says Tony—tells her, "No, I'm sorry, ma'am, but there are only four riders allowed per vehicle. To accommodate five, you would need two vehicles, but the tour is completely sold out for today, so I do not have an extra vehicle."

I just stand there, fighting back the tears. It was stupid to have gotten my hopes up. Tony looks like he feels sorry for me. She just embarrassed me right here in public and now I get to sit in the car alone for the next three hours. I won't let myself cry in front of this terrible woman. I should have known this was too good to be true. Uncle Dan looks pissed. I'm not sure why. He's never shown any interest in me before, so why now does he care that I am not included.

I speak up, "It's all right. I'll wait in the car." My voice cracks at the end. Uncle Dan opens his mouth to go off but gets cut off.

I feel a tug on the back of my shirt and a body walks past my left side.

"She can ride with me, Tony." I hear from a familiar voice.

I turn my head to see the guy from the beach last night. He is wearing a bright green shirt like Tony. His name tag says Ethan. He too is holding a clipboard, collecting signatures. I must have overlooked him in the crowd when we first arrived.

"All right. You're with Ethan. I just need your name and signature here please." Tony seems surprised but nods his head and directs me where to sign, then takes his clipboard back.

"Go ahead and follow him up there."

I am speechless. I was about to sit in a hot, muggy car for three hours, when a knight in shining armor comes to my rescue. *Why would he let me ride with him?* I look at my family. Aunt Susan seems irritated that I get to go anyway despite her sabotage. Uncle Dan is staring daggers into the side of her head. Sam has his nose glued into his phone and Denise is primping herself in her camera.

"I guess I'll be with him." I leave them to go stand with Ethan.

"Hi," I say quietly as I approach him from the crowd.

He smiles. "Hi again."

He turns to speak to the crowd of riders. "*Aloha*, everyone! My name is Ethan and I am one of your tour leaders today. We also have Jeremy and Liam over there who will be trailing with us. Jeremy will take the lead, I will be in the middle, and Liam will bring up the rear. Please keep your helmets on at all times, unless we are outside of our vehicles. It is muddy out there today, so be thankful you didn't wear white." I notice him as he shoots a dirty look toward Denise. "Go slow, we are in no rush, and pay close attention to the ATV in front of you. We don't need any accidents today. Everyone, please load into your assigned vehicles. We will get moving shortly. Please stay in a single file line as we exit the driveway. Have fun and *aloha*!"

He finishes his spiel with a *shaka* and motions for me to follow him. We walk over to the bright green employee ATV and he hands me a helmet.

"Safety first. I'm Ethan, by the way," he says, holding out his hand.

"Zoey," I reply, shaking it. I strap the helmet under my chin and can't help feeling like a little kid.

"Hop in." He points to the passenger seat of his ATV. Jeremy leads the line of ATVs out of the driveway. After six regular ATVs, Tony stops the line to allow us to exit, then motions for the others to follow after us.

I sit quietly, thinking about what Aunt Susan did. I don't understand what I have done wrong. That was one of the most embarrassing moments I have ever felt. I feel like no one wants me around. I didn't mean to be put into their family. It's not my fault my parents died. A tear slips out of the corner of my eye on accident, my emotions getting to me. I feel Ethan's fingers brush against my knee. I quickly wipe the tear off my cheek, giving him a fake smile.

"So, from what I witnessed, I take it you and your mom don't get along?"

"Not my mom, but no, we don't. She's my aunt," I scoff.

"Where's your mom?"

"She and my dad died in a car crash three years ago."

"Shit. I'm sorry. I shouldn't have asked."

"No, it's all right. I'm used to it," I tell him. Unfortunately, that's true. I always get asked about my parents.

There's a brief pause before he dives back into his questions.

"Does she always treat you like that?"

I laugh a little. "Pretty much. It's basically a Cinderella story. Instead of an evil stepmother and nasty stepsisters, I have two snotty cousins and an aunt preventing any form of happiness."

"So, I would assume you'd like to not be around them right

now?"

"You assume correctly. It's only eleven a.m. and I have had all I can take from them."

"Got it." I'm confused. What can he do about me not wanting to be around my family right now? He's all up in my business but for some reason, I don't seem to mind sharing these details with him. It's nice having someone to talk to. He radios to the other guys.

"You boys, good by yourself for a while?" he asks over the radio.

"Of course. Is something up?" Jeremy responds.

"I'm taking a detour to the *wailele*."

I hear a bunch of howls come back over the radio.

"All right, man, we got this. Go have fun with the girl," Liam responds.

I notice Ethan turn the volume down on the radio.

"What's *wailele*?" I ask, feeling like I am being kidnapped but also not minding it.

"You'll see." He gives me that cheeky grin of his. We get to a split in the path where you can go left or right. The tour group takes the left path but Ethan turns down the right one. He throws the ATV in park, jumping out to motion for the other vehicles to follow the group, not us. Smart. My family is in the second to last ATV, glaring us down as they drive up. My uncle stops their ATV and asks where we are going.

"She's riding with me, but unfortunately I have to check on some maintenance on another path so we will meet up with you and the rest of the group after lunch."

That seems good enough for my uncle, so my family drives off and Ethan jumps back in our ATV.

"Are we seriously going to do maintenance work?" I ask, not

looking forward to that.

"Of course not, but I didn't want them getting any ideas to follow us."

I smile. He catches on quick. That's my type of thinking there.

We drive in silence for a while, watching as the forest fills with vegetation, vines getting denser. We keep going until all of the trees block out the sun, making it feel chillier than it is. I'm getting kind of sketched out riding with a man I just met into the middle of the woods, but he did tell his coworkers where we were going, so he must not be planning to kill me.

"Don't sweat. I'm not luring you into the woods to murder you. We are almost there."

Damn, it's like he can read my thoughts. Just like that the trees break apart, revealing a beam of sunlight glistening on a large waterfall. He parks the ATV, instantly jumping out to walk closer to the waterfall. I notice there is a sign posted in red '*KAPU*,' Ethan explains that it says 'keep out' but that he's allowed to be here. The mist off the waterfall is refracting in the light creating a small rainbow over the pool of water at the bottom. The sight is magical—all of the clear water sparkling like diamonds as it pours over the cliff edge.

"*Wailele* means waterfall."

"It's beautiful," I reply. I have never seen something so magnificent.

"So are you," he says casually walking past me. I almost didn't hear him.

"What?" I gasp.

He turns back to look at me. "I said you are beautiful. It's a compliment. You should learn to take one." He laughs. He's confident and cocky.

I stand there, shocked. "Didn't you hear my aunt earlier telling me to suck it in?"

"I heard, she seems like an *ilio wahine* if you ask me."

"I'm not sure what that means, but okay."

"It means she's a bitch."

His words stun me for a second before I start laughing uncontrollably. No one has ever had the nerve to say that about my aunt out loud before. "That's great."

He smiles, clearly amused at my hysteria. He keeps walking to the bottom of the waterfall with me trailing close behind him. When we get to the sandy embankment he starts unbuttoning his pants.

"*Woah!* What are you doing?" I shriek, covering my eyes.

"Going for a swim." Laughing at me, he pulls his shirt over his head. I can't stop myself from checking out his torso. The black swirls over his bicep are a huge turn on. He catches me staring and chuckles. He runs up the embankment behind me and unties a rope that was wrapped around a tree. He is about to rope swing into a waterfall. *What kind of fantasy did I fall into?*

He jumps holding onto the rope, then lets go when he is above the water. He does a freaking backflip. I watch him resurface, shaking the water from his hair. There are water droplets on his eyelashes and it makes my body feel like melting into the depths of his eyes.

"Are you just going to stare at me or are you going to jump?" he yells.

This has to be unsafe. This is beyond the fathoms of my protective bubble. This is something my parents would do, not me. Yet here I am, stripping down to my bra and panties, getting ready to rope swing into a waterfall, with a mysterious boy I just met. I feel his eyes on my body as I undress. I'm not fat but I am also not skinny. I put on a little weight after the accident, eating constantly in an attempt to numb the pain. I feel self-conscious but I am too far now to turn back. I climb up to the rope and wrap both hands around it tightly, screaming as my feet lift off of the ground. I am too scared to let go so I swing back over the beach. The second time around he yells for me to let go and I do. I plummet into the cold water beneath me. He is waiting for me as I break the surface.

"Are you okay?" he asks.

"That was awesome!" I yell. "I've never done anything like that. This is what they were always talking about!"

"Who?"

"My parents. They used to tell me stories about the adventures they'd go on. They swam with sharks, cliff-dived, jumped out of airplanes. You name it, they did it. I passed up so many opportunities because I thought they were reckless and dangerous but that, right now, was the most amazing adrenaline rush I have ever experienced."

"Your parents sound like badass people."

"They were." I smile, feeling elated with their memory and adrenaline.

"Come on, I want to show you something," he says. I follow him through the waterfall into a hidden cave. It's dark, with little sun shining through. Stalactites are hanging from the ceiling and the water is cooler in this area. My skin pricks in goosebumps. A person would never be able to tell this cave was here just from looking at the waterfall.

"Wow! This is amazing," I tell him.

"This is my secret spot. No one knows about this cave but me. And now, you."

"Oh, sure. I'm sure you tell all the ladies that, when you

bring them here to have your way with them," I say sarcastically, not falling for his line.

He looks amused as he shakes his head. "I don't bring ladies here to have my way with them. I come here to think."

"How'd you find this place?"

"*Uh,* my father was in a motorcycle accident three years ago. A drunk driver swerved into his lane and hit him head-on. He broke his neck, seven vertebrae in his spine, and both legs. He was hospitalized for two years. When it first happened, I didn't know how to cope. One day, I had a breakdown and took off into these woods. I found this waterfall and decided to jump in. When I found this cave, I felt safe, so I hid in here for hours, falling apart. When I calmed down, I went home to find my mother franticly calling everyone trying to find me. She was so relieved to see me. I felt so bad for scaring her."

"I'm so sorry," I say sincerely.

"It's in the past now. He's alive. He is paralyzed from the neck down, permanently confined to a wheelchair. He went to court and won a large settlement. That's how I have your dream Jeep. My parents bought it for me for my seventeenth birthday after they received the money. We were pretty broke before that. They paid off our house and we were able to pay all of my dad's medical bills."

I don't know what to do so I swim over to him, wrapping my arms around his neck. "I'm sorry."

"It's okay. I didn't want you to feel sorry for me. I just wanted you to know how I found the cave."

"I love the cave. I love the *wailele*," I say in Hawaiian, which feels foreign on my tongue but nice. He chuckles.

"Are you cold?" he asks.

"Not really, why?" I am cold but I don't want him to know

that.

"I can feel your nipples against my chest." He laughs. I turn red and swim backward away from him. *How can he possibly feel that through my padding?*

"Let's head back." He saves me from having to say anything.

When we make it back to the shore, he seems uncomfortable.

"Is everything okay?" I ask, worried about the change in him.

"Can you not mention what I told you in the cave to anyone? I've never really talked about that before. And maybe not tell anyone about the cave? Please?"

"What happens in the cave stays in the cave," I say trying to lighten the mood. "Thank you for sharing."

"You're easy to talk to. You seem to get it."

I smile. We get dressed and walk back up to the ATV. We have been gone for a while now. The lunch break is about over. We need to meet back up with the group. He pulls a bag of snacks from the back compartment.

"Sorry we missed lunch," he says apologetically.

"Don't be. Being here with you was better than any lunch." His eyes seem to brighten upon hearing that.

He hands me an individual loaf of banana bread and mini bottle of water, taking one of each for himself. We snack as he drives us to the meeting point. When we pull into the group, everyone has finished lunch and is piling back into their ATVs. His coworkers Liam and Jeremy are wearing big shit-eating grins on their faces when they notice we have arrived. Ethan's cheeks flush a bit. Denise is walking past us but stops.

"Did you two go swimming?" she asks, noticing how wet we are. Ethan looks over to me, unsure of how to respond. Thinking quickly, I tell her the first thing that pops into my head,

"Not exactly. I fell into the river trying to help with the maintenance. He had to jump in and save me."

She cackles, "Of course, you did. You're such a klutz. I'm sorry you got stuck riding with her. If you want, I'll switch with her and you can enjoy my company for the rest of the trip." She's flirting with him! Right in front of me!

"Actually, I'll stick with her. I'm not sure if I could drive far with your smell making my eyes water. Did they take you guys through the manure fields?" he asks back, fanning his hand in front of his nose.

My jaw hits the ground. No one has ever turned down Denise like that. Especially not for me. She looks like she's just been slapped. She storms off to my family waiting in their ATV. I see her sneak a spritz of perfume from her purse.

"No one has ever turned down Denise. You are my hero! Did you see her face? That was incredible!"

"I won't listen to her insult you in front of me, plus she is definitely not my type. Who dresses like that for an off-roading trip through the forest? That's ridiculous!"

"She's a flirt. Always on the hunt for her next guy. Can't keep the same boyfriend for more than a week," I tell him.

"And how long can you keep a boyfriend?" he asks smoothly.

"Don't know. Never had one," I tell him honestly.

He looks surprised when I tell him this. He's about to ask another question when Liam and Jeremy approach, still looking like mischievous cats.

"Hey, you two. Have fun in the *wailele*?" They laugh.

Ethan turns red. If he can stick up for me, I can do the same for him.

"Absolutely, but if you find my panties, can I get them back?

They were my favorite pair."

The color drains from Ethan's face as his head twists to stare at me. I'm pretty sure he just got whiplash. Liam and Jeremy look terrified by the image of us doing it in the waterfall. I burst out laughing. They join in when they realize it's a joke.

"This chick is cool. She's got balls," they say, giving me a fist bump.

Ethan looks relieved. I can be unexpected at times.

"Are we ready to roll?" Liam asks.

"Yeah, let's head back. I'll jump back in the middle," Ethan tells them.

Jeremy leads the group away from the lookout point. We pull into the line after the sixth ATV just like before but this time, my family pulls out right behind us. Denise is driving.

"For the love of God," I say out loud.

"What?" he asks.

"Look behind us." He looks in the rearview mirror. "Seriously?" he asks, sounding annoyed.

"I will buy you dinner if you hit every mud puddle on the way out of here and blast them," I offer, not realizing I have just implied a date.

He looks intrigued. "Deal."

As we drive back to the lodge, Ethan rams our vehicle through every inch of mud, covering both of us as well as my family behind us. Especially Denise. She is never going to get the mud stains out of her white clothes. Her shorts are going to look like someone had explosive diarrhea all over her. We get stuck in a particularly deep puddle, so he floors the gas pedal sending a shower of mud behind us until we are freed. He looks like he is enjoying this. We make it back to the main grounds, drenched in wet dirt.

"So, what time should I pick you up tonight?" he asks confidently with splatters all over his face, knowing he did an amazing job at mudding my family.

I let out a small laugh. "Is six all right?"

"Six is perfect. Give me your phone," he says.

I awkwardly hand him my phone, unsure as to why he wants it.

"Here," he says, handing it back. He put his phone number in it and texted himself so he would have my number too. "Text me the address you're staying at."

I do it immediately, not wanting to forget. My heart is racing. I just got a guy's number and am going on a date tonight!

Slowly, I climb out of the little bubble we have created in his ATV, not wanting to burst the feeling. I hear my family in the distance throwing a fit about all the mud they were covered in.

"Zoey, come on or we are leaving without you. I need to wash this mud out of my hair before it dries." I hear my aunt yell at me.

He scrunches his face with the way she talked to me. "I guess I will see you later tonight then," I tell him as I start to back away.

"It's a date." He smiles back.

I head to our rental car. I already know the interior is about to get destroyed. I turn back to see him watching me. I smile and wave, climbing in the car. The ride back is full of Aunt Susan and Denise complaining about all the mud. My uncle looks disgusted by the whole day, Samson doesn't even read in this car ride, for fear of getting his anatomy book covered with mud.

When we get back to the house, Denise and Aunt Susan run off to be the first ones in the shower. To be kind, I offer my shower to Uncle Dan and Samson. Samson grabs his shower kit and heads into my room. I grab a seat at the kitchen island while

Uncle Dan pours himself a double shot of whiskey.

"I have a date tonight," I tell him, surprising even myself. I guess I felt the need to tell him since I won't be around tonight. I didn't want them to expect to have to take me out with them.

He raises his eyebrows at me. "Your first date? You're responsible enough and we are on vacation so I don't see a reason to instate a curfew. Have fun."

"Thanks. I will," I reply happily. I head off to check out my wardrobe to see what I could possibly wear for a date. I don't want to be too dressy but I want to look amazing after how he saw me today.

Chapter 6

After spending a generous amount of time shampooing my hair, washing away clumps of dirt, I decide to braid it down my back. My mom taught me how to braid my hair when I was nine. It makes me look a few years older this way. I brought several dresses with me for the ease of wearing them over a swimsuit. I choose a sky blue one. It's tight around my chest making my breasts really stand out and then it flows out below that. It has miniature dark blue flowers set against the sky blue back ground. It's one of my favorites and makes me look really hot. I strap on the silver sandals I bought for this trip knowing that I suck in heels. They crisscross around my calf up to my knee like an Egyptian. I splurged on myself when I went shopping before coming here knowing I had nothing nice to wear. I apply some light blue glittery eye shadow that matches perfectly. Thankfully, I brought my makeup bag, even though I haven't used it in almost three years. This is the first time I have put time into my appearance in who knows how long. It feels good, like a glimpse of the person I used to be. I add my finishing touches: some shiny lip gloss, silver earrings, my mother's necklace. A cloud of perfume later, I am ready to go. Just in time too. Ethan should be here any minute.

I walk out into the living room where Samson gives me a surprised look.

"Why do you look somewhat decent?" he remarks.

"Thanks. I will take that as a compliment. I have a date," I tell him.

Denise walks out and sees me. She starts laughing. "What's got you so dressed up?" Of course, she has to make fun of me. I should have escaped out my bedroom door.

"She has a date," my uncle tells her, walking into the room from behind her. "And she looks nice," he says in my direction.

Wow! He said I look nice. That makes me happy. I tell him thanks, and then there is a knock on the door. Ethan. Time to flaunt this in front of Denise.

I open the door to see Ethan in a dark blue button-down that accents the tan of his skin. Somehow, we have managed to color coordinate our outfits without even talking about it. His hair is gelled up and spikey. His eyes dilate with his mouth hanging open. "Fuck," he whispers. He immediately blushes and apologizes. I laugh and let him in. Denise looks like she saw a ghost.

"YOU are going out with HIM?" she yells in shock.

I grin at her. "Yep," Ethan says beside me.

"Why in the hell would you go out with her?" she squeals.

"Have you not showered yet? You should really get on that before you stink up the whole house." He shoots at her. I love this. She squeals and runs off with smoke coming out of her ears. I even see my uncle hide a smile behind his whiskey glass.

"Have fun, you two," he tells us and walks out of the room.

"Come on, let's get going," I say as I turn to walk out the door. He follows behind me. When we get to his Jeep, he opens my door and offers me his hand for balance to step up inside.

"You *nani' oe*," he comments as I climb inside.

"What's that mean?" I ask, loving the sound of his native language

"Beautiful."

"You look pretty handsome yourself." I flash him a smile. He closes my door and jumps in the driver seat. "So, what do you feel like eating?" he asks.

"Well, I had fish last night. So maybe a burger tonight?" I respond.

He smiles. "I know a place with great burgers."

He drives us about twenty minutes to this cute little burger joint. It has a big burger sign that says Smoking Patties. We get a table on the patio and order a couple of waters.

"Please don't order a salad," he tells me, almost worried, as I look over the menu.

"Why would I? They have a pineapple cheeseburger! I fully plan to experience everything Hawaiian." I laugh, embarrassing myself with my love of food.

"Every time I have gone out with a girl, all they order is a salad and it's annoying. I want someone who can eat."

"So, you're saying we need to order mozzarella sticks too?" I give him my best smile.

"Yeah, that sounds good." He seems happy with that.

When the server comes back, I order the Poppin Pineapple burger that has pineapple and jalapeño on it. I request no veggies. My view on lettuce is that it takes away from the flavor of the burger. If I want watery lettuce, I'll order a salad. Ethan orders the Jumping Jack which has pepper jack cheese, bacon, and BBQ sauce. Of course, we get an order of mozzarella sticks.

"So how did the rest of work go?" I ask him, knowing he had another tour after mine today.

"It wasn't quite as eventful as your tour," he chuckles. "It was the usual."

"How long have you worked there?"

"A little over three years. I started when I was fifteen. I just

41

started leading the tours when I turned eighteen last December. My uncle requires everyone to be at least eighteen to drive the ATVs."

"Your uncle?"

"Yeah, Tony, he's my uncle."

"Oh, that's cool. He seems like a pretty chill guy. Especially since he let me ride with you today when my aunt sabotaged the reservation."

"He's very laid back. It's nice working with him."

Our mozzarella sticks arrive and we reach for one at the same time, our hands brushing.

"Sorry," he says.

"Don't be," I say.

The mozzarella is super melty and cheesy. I try not to be an animal as I inhale it. I have to remind myself to breathe between bites. When our burgers show up, I groan. It looks delicious, with cheese dripping down the side and a large side of fries. I heavily salt mine and squirt some ketchup off to the side. He drizzles the ketchup on top of his fries, murdering them.

"Oh no," I say out loud.

"What's wrong?" he asks, worried.

"I don't know if this can work with you eating soggy fries like that. Dipping is the way to go." I smile, letting him know that I'm kidding.

He laughs and pops a fry in his mouth.

"They are not soggy; they warm up the ketchup and absorb the flavor." I grimace.

"No. That is a crime against food." I laugh.

I bite into my burger. "Oh my god. It's like an orgasm in my mouth." He blushes at my word choice.

"I was hoping you would like it."

We eat in silence, both of us having missed lunch. When we are down to the last few fries, I notice he has BBQ sauce on the side of his mouth. I smile at him.

"What?" He notices me staring.

"Hold still," I tell him. I swipe my thumb across his bottom lip catching the BBQ sauce. Without thinking, I suck my thumb, noticing him staring at me, eyes wide.

"Sorry, you had BBQ sauce on your lip," I explain.

"That was extremely hot," he tells me. Now it's my turn to blush. The server brings the check and before I can grab it, he hands his card to the lady, who walks away with it.

"Hey! I was supposed to buy YOU dinner, remember? You saved my ass today."

"You can buy dessert," he offers. Not good enough, but I'll settle for that for now until I can make it up to him.

"Fine, but you better order a quadruple scoop ice cream or something," I joke. When the server returns his card, he signs the slip, leaving a twenty-five percent tip then we stand to leave. He's a good tipper too!

We walk through the town, browsing through the little shops, full of souvenirs and tourist traps. There's a tattoo shop and I think to myself how cool it would be to get a tattoo in Hawaii. He takes me into this surf store that smells like marijuana, he apparently knows the owner. Several people greet him, giving him high fives, shoving his shoulder. I can see that Ethan is a pretty popular guy.

"Have you ever been surfing?" he asks.

"There's not a lot of surfing in Michigan," I joke.

"Would you want to learn?"

"I'll try anything once," I respond but it sounded dirtier out loud. "I am done playing it safe. From today forward I plan to live my life to the fullest, just like my parents." Something changed when I entered that waterfall, a new, adventurous side of me has awoken.

"Can I help you with that?" he asks.

"I hope so. I have a lot on my to-do list."

"Are you free tomorrow morning? It's my day off. I can give you your first surf lesson."

"Well since it is clear that I am not wanted by my family, I will have to plan my own activities so I think I can pencil you in tomorrow," I joke.

He smiles. "I'll pick you up at seven a.m. then."

We walk into an ice cream parlor. They have ice cream, sorbet, and lots of gelato. There are over twenty flavors and I have a hard time deciding. Ethan chooses the tiramisu gelato and I decide on the Almond Joy since I am pretty much addicted to anything coconut. I make sure to be at the register first when they ring us up. I block the card swipe so I am guaranteed to buy our dessert. He laughs and thanks me. We take our gelato and walk across the street onto the beach. We sit in the sand just out of reach of the waves.

"You like coffee? I ask him.

"Yeah, I am a big coffee drinker. Lots of early mornings," he tells me.

"I like coffee too. The restaurant I work in makes their own tiramisu and it's my favorite."

"Here try this." He holds a spoonful of tiramisu gelato in front of me. It's awkward taking the bite off his spoon while he watches me.

"That is so much better than work," I tell him. I load up my spoon and hold it to his lips.

"You like coconut?" I ask.

44

"I'm Hawaiian. I kind of have to." He laughs and swallows the gelato off my spoon. I am turned on watching him lick the ice cream off his lip. I lick my own lips involuntarily. He doesn't notice so I go back to eating my gelato watching the waves. The sun is beginning to set on the horizon. When we finish, he asks if I want to take a walk. I say sure and he gently entwines our fingers, helping me up from the sand. We deposit our plastic containers in the recycling bin before we begin our walk. We walk the beach, kicking our shoes off, carrying them in our free hands. We keep the topics light as we talk, knowing we both have a lot of darkness in our lives. After talking about our childhoods for a while, he changes the topic.

"So, what is first on your list?"

I realize he is talking about my 'living' list. Or I guess you could call it a bucket list. After the tour this morning, I spent time compiling a list of activities I want to try before my time comes to leave this earth.

"Well, rope swing got checked off this morning. I can check off first date now. And surfing will be crossed off tomorrow. I don't know. What do you suggest?"

He stops walking and stares at me. "First date?" he asks in disbelief.

I laugh. "Yeah. I told you earlier I've never had a boyfriend. This is my first date. I was fifteen when my parents died and after that, I shut myself off from the rest of the world. I don't have the normal teenage milestones checked off."

He just looks at me bewildered. I can't tell if he feels sad for me or if he is holding back from asking another question.

"To save you from having to ask, because I can see what you're thinking: no, I have never been kissed, obviously I'm a virgin, I've never been to a party or done any kind of drug, or drank alcohol. I know that's not normal, so if you would like to leave now, I understand." I am honest but confident with him. If he doesn't want someone like me then we should stop wasting our time. I can't read him now. I have no idea what he is thinking, as he just stares at me, absorbing this new information. I look out to the waves to let him process. He walks closer to me, chests rising against each other's. He cups my cheek in his hand, tilting my head so I am staring directly into his green orbs.

"Can I be your first kiss?" he asks softly. All I can manage is a nod. He gently brushes his lips across mine. So tender yet engulfing. His lips consume mine, evaporating the air from my lungs. I can taste the espresso from the gelato, encouraging me to deepen the kiss further. I part my lips, and he cautiously slides his tongue against mine. He feels rigid as if he's waiting for my reaction. I slide my hands over his chest until I reach his neck and press my hands against each side, holding his face to mine. I smooth my tongue across his, feeling him relax. In an attempt to be sexy, I suck his bottom lip between my teeth, biting gently.

He's the first to pull away, both of us breathing heavily. "Are you sure that was your first kiss?" he asks, rubbing a finger across his lips. I'm still breathless so I give him a little nod, pulling my hands away from his neck. I step back and clear my throat.

"So, it doesn't bother you that I'm… inexperienced?" I ask him shyly. Embarrassed about all the intimate details I let him in on.

"Not at all. If I'm being honest, it makes me want to be the one who you experience those firsts with."

"Come on. We should keep walking before we cross anything else off my list," I tell him.

He quirks his eyebrow at me but grabs my hand to keep walking.

"So, what is on your list of adventures?" he asks, hopeful.

Having given this some thought throughout the day, I respond, "Cliff diving, helicopter ride, snorkeling, I want to get a tattoo, and go bungee jumping. Skinny dipping seems like a regular teenage experience to endure. I want to hike the Haleakala crater. Maybe visit the Great Wall of China and the reefs in Australia like my parents."

"That's an awesome list."

"I want to experience everything," I tell him.

We walk back to his Jeep, and again he opens my door and offers to help me in. The drive home is less awkward. I feel more myself. I turn on his radio and we listen to some local Hawaiian band as background music. He holds my hand the entire way back to my place. We pull in and he turns off the car. He gives me his million-dollar smile.

"I had an amazing time with you tonight," he says.

I blush. "It was perfect. Thank you for dinner."

"Thank you for dessert." With the way he is looking at me, I don't think he's talking about the gelato.

He gets out and opens my door. I slide out, staring into his eyes until my feet hit the ground. He walks me to the door, as if this were some old-fashioned, romantic movie. It makes my heart flutter. I am a hopeless romantic for all of those old-timey love stories. When we are right in front of the door, I turn to look at him, hoping for another kiss. He smiles, stepping closer, seemingly sensing what I want. He tucks a strand of my hair that has come free of its braid behind my ear.

"Goodnight," he whispers then presses his lips against mine. I savor this kiss. It has to last me at least until tomorrow. No tongue is involved this time, just the innocent press of lips on lips. I feel like my heart is going to beat out of my chest. I pull

47

away, knowing we've been standing here for several minutes.

"Goodnight," I whisper back to him. I watch as he walks to his Jeep and backs out of the drive. I open the door and walk into the kitchen with a dopey smile on my face, only to jump out of my skin when I find my uncle standing in the kitchen.

"You scared me," I say clutching my chest.

"How was your date?" he asks calmly. It's strange interacting with him, almost as if he cares about me. He usually keeps quiet, going along with whatever my aunt says.

"It was nice. We are going surfing in the morning," I tell him so he knows I'll be gone tomorrow as well.

"Thanks for the heads up. I'm going to bed now," he states, walking to his room.

"Wait," I call. "Did you wait up for me to get home?"

"I wanted to make sure you got home okay," he says and continues walking. He shuts the door to his and my aunt's room, signaling our discussion is over. *Strange,* I thought. *He wanted to make sure I was okay?* He barely speaks to me most of the time. We come to Hawaii and all of a sudden, he takes an interest in me. I don't dwell on it too long, still in the after-date bliss, I head to my room and collapse on my bed, still wearing my dress. I untie my sandals, brush my hair out so it doesn't knot through the night, and slip into my pajama shorts and one of Dad's t-shirts. I snuggle into my covers, checking my phone one last time before going to bed. I have a single text message. Ethan. I smile as I open it: 8 hours until I see you again. I smile, finding it adorable that he is counting the hours.

Not soon enough, I reply. I set my phone on the nightstand to charge and finally relax in the sheets. I close my eyes and let the night replay in my head. Eight hours.

Chapter 7

I wake up at six a.m., heart pounding with the thought of seeing Ethan in an hour. I jump in the shower to get my hair wet so I can gel it today. I apply a coat of eyeliner and mascara, calling it good. My swimsuit consists of a black, ruffled bottom that covers my stomach, hiding my insecurities, while the top is basically a push up bra but it's covered in purple sequins and makes my chest look double its natural size. I hope Ethan will like it. I have about ten minutes until he's supposed to be here so I quietly sneak into the kitchen and make some Nutella toast with a glass of milk. When I am done, I decide to wait in the garage bay so I don't wake anyone up. I pace back and forth, checking the time on my phone. Suddenly, I see a flash of bright orange. As soon as he is up the driveway, I climb in, shutting my door silently.

"Good morning," he says. His hair is wet as if he just got out of the shower. He's wearing a pair of black swim trunks that make him look even more deeply tanned. He's also wearing his signature *slippahs* that I have learned is what they call flip-flops here in Hawai'i.

"Morning," I say back with a smile.

"How did you sleep?" he asks, backing out of the driveway.

"Peacefully. It was the best sleep I have had in a long time," I tell him.

He smiles. "Good."

We drive to the beach in silence, watching the beginning of sunrise, allowing ourselves to slowly wake up. Looking around the vehicle, I spot two surfboards strapped to the top. I also notice some snorkel gear in the back seat. I catch a glimpse of a picnic basket which puts butterflies in my belly with the thought of having a beach picnic with him after our surfing lesson. When we get to his favorite surfing spot, he works on undoing the straps to the surfboards. His shirt raises with his arms, drawing my attention to a small strip of hair beginning at his belly button, trailing down into his trunks. He jumps down with a cocky grin, letting me know he caught me staring at him again, and hands me the larger of the two boards. From my newfound surf knowledge I researched yesterday, I know that beginner boards are large to make balance easier and they get smaller as your skills develop. As we get to the shore and he lays his board in the sand motioning for me to do the same.

"We are going to start in the sand until you feel stable enough to go in the water," he explains.

"All right," I say. Maybe I won't make a complete fool of myself.

"Step on the board with your dominant foot." I step with my right foot first, following his instructions. "Arms out to keep your balance." I raise my arms out from my sides. "Now slightly bend your knees. That's great. Perfect form. Now slowly rotate your torso around keeping your core centered." I twist around, flailing my arms as I lose my balance. I am so not doing this right.

"Here," he says stepping off his board, coming to stand behind me. He wraps his arm around my midsection, placing his hand flat against my ribs. "Hold still here but move from this area," he says holding my core center but turning my outer body. I try to concentrate on the motions but I also feel his warmth against my back, his breath against my neck. "There you go."

"I have a good instructor," I say, noticing him look away at the compliment. He goes back to his board, picking it up from the sand.

"Do you feel okay to try it in the water?"

"Sure!" I say excited to finally get in the water. I pull my swimsuit cover over my head and kick my sandals aside. He's staring at me. "Woah," he says.

"You okay?" I ask with a hint of amusement.

"Your um… I like your, uh… swimsuit. It looks really good," he stutters.

"I showed you mine, now show me yours," I giggle noticing he is still wearing his shirt. He blushes and throws his board down. Now it's my turn to stare. He laughs as I make no attempt to shield my view.

"God, I want to lick your abs," I say out loud. My eyes go wide as realization hits me. "I didn't mean to say that out loud." I try to cover, but it's too late. He's got a shit-eating grin on his face, his eyes dark with desire. "I'm going to go surf," I announce running into the ocean. He jogs behind me, catching up. When we get in the water he instructs me to put the board on the surface and lay on top of it. I do so, feeling his eyes on my ass as I lay down.

Clearing his throat, he says, "Now paddle." We paddle out until he says hold up. I sit up on my board like I've done this before. "Nice job," he tells me. I smile at my accomplishment. He rests his hand on the surface of the water, staring out at the horizon. "Now we wait for a wave," he tells me.

As we sit on our boards taking in the calm serenity that is the ocean, I can't help but wonder why Ethan is here with me. It's not like I live here, nothing serious could ever happen between us. And I am definitely not as pretty as the other girls I see on the beach. The question slips out of my mouth before I

51

can restrain myself.

"Why are you here with me?" I say, feeling this is all too good to be true.

He looks at me, contemplating.

"I mean, I'm nothing special. I'm just an orphan girl from Michigan, dragged along on my family's vacation. Why waste your time with me when I'm only here for a few days?"

He looks deep in thought as he replies, "I can't explain it, I feel drawn to you. Like we've been friends our whole lives."

"Oh. I thought maybe it was just pity," I reply, looking down at my board.

"Not at all. I do hate the way your family treats you, but that's not why I asked you out here with me. I want to learn more about you. It's like finding a seashell on the beach, something new and unique to explore on a coast of boring sand grains."

"Oh, I don't think I can live up to seashell qualities," I joke, feeling self-conscious.

"Why not? You're beautiful and tough in your natural form, just like a seashell."

"Thanks." I smile, basking in the compliment.

"Come on. You gotta catch at least one wave," he tells me, preparing for a big swell rolling in.

I paddle my heart out, managing to stand up and keep my balance till I hit the shoreline and don't know how to stop. I fall off, into the sand dying with laughter. I watch as Ethan shreds a wave, doing all sorts of twists and turns, riding the full force of the wave back into the beach. It's hot to watch. I'm sitting in the sand beside my board as he comes over.

"Are you all right?" he asks.

"I am fantastic!" I say jumping up, ready to try again. This time I do better at keeping my core centered. I twist my hips jerking the board and manage my own little trick on the wave. Nothing like Ethan's, but it gives me satisfaction. We surf until the sun is directly overhead and take a break for lunch.

He fetches the picnic basket from the car, opening it to reveal a variety of fresh foods. There is some banana bread, strawberries, pineapple, a container with hamburger buns in it. Ethan pulls out a metal box and opens the lid. It is full of steaming hot pork, the smell makes my stomach growl. He also pulls out two glass bottles of water.

"Wow, this looks amazing," I say, looking over everything.

He makes me a sandwich of the pulled pork. When I take a bite, juices flood my taste buds, so savory yet sweet, with a hint of spice in the afterbite. It is delicious. I moan as I chew letting him know how much I am enjoying this.

"Who made this pulled pork? It is the best meat I have ever put in my mouth."

He chokes on his water with my comment. I laugh, knowing I caught him off guard. "I did," he tells me.

"You made this? It is outstanding," I say, taking another large bite.

"I'm glad you like it. I make my own BBQ sauce." He laughs.

We munch on pulled pork sandwiches and fruit. I even try the *musubi* he offers me. It's spam and rice wrapped in seaweed, kind of like sushi but without the fish. I've never been a fan of spam but the way it is seasoned in the wrap makes me think that I could eat lots more of them. I finish with a piece of banana bread that is even more delicious than the one from the ATV tour. "Did you make the bread too?" I question him.

He blushes knowing another compliment is coming.

"Damn. You can seriously cook."

"This is nothing," he states.

"Well, to me it's heavenly. I'm used to getting a meal that costs less than five dollars through some drive-thru. My aunt is a terrible cook. Even if she does manage to cook something edible, she always makes comments about what I eat or how I eat it, so I try not to eat when she's around," I say sadly.

"You should never feel bad for eating anything. I wish I could cook for you every day," he tells me.

When we are done, he packs everything away in the picnic basket, returning it to the backseat of the Jeep. I lay back in the sand enjoying the scorching rays of the sun.

"Ready to go snorkeling?" he asks after the sun has dried all the water off our bodies.

"Really? We're going snorkeling?" I ask surprised.

"Yep, we're crossing another item off your list." I am just now noticing that he has the snorkels and masks in his hands.

He helps me adjust the mask over my face, leaving the snorkel out of my mouth until we get in the water.

"Sexy, huh?" I ask giving him a goofy look in my mask.

"Everything you wear is sexy." He winks. We work our way out slowly, observing all the rocks and corals.

With my head under the water, the world goes silent. I see blues, greens, and browns of every shade. The water is as clear as crystal, allowing me the privilege to gaze into the depths below. I see a yellow brain coral on the ocean floor. There is a school of mahi-mahi swimming past. Ethan points out a *Humuhumunukunukuapua'a* causing me to squeal in touristy delight at seeing the state fish of Hawaii. As we swim deeper, we spot three green sea turtles, or *honu* as Ethan calls them, floating by a pile of rocks. I keep my distance, remembering Ethan mentioning that they are a protected species. Moving closer to the coral to see tiny fish swimming through the porous holes, I lift my arm to maneuver around a large piece sticking out, when suddenly, I can't move. My sequin top is stuck in the coral. Luckily, I am close enough to the surface I can raise my head for a breath of air. I grab my breast and jerk hoping to free myself without Ethan noticing. I think it gets even more stuck though. I rock my side back and forth hoping to break it free, only to avail with a scrape against my ribcage. Ethan swims up to me, noticing my absence from the depths below.

"Everything okay?" he asks, worried.

"Oh yeah. Everything is great. Just sticking to the coral," I say trying to pass myself off as calm, cool, and collected. I have my arm over my chest trying to unravel the part that is stuck when he notices me pulling on my top.

"Are you actually stuck?" he asks, finding it to be hilarious.

"No," I say coolly. "I just really like this spot." Trying to appear as if I don't need help.

"Oh okay." He grins, seeing right through my bullshit.

I resign. "Fine, I'm stuck."

He laughs. "Let me take a look." He puts his mask back on, ducking under the surface. I feel his fingers rub against mine, fighting with the material. I try not to think about how close his face is to my breast right now. He resurfaces.

"I promise I am not trying to get you naked at the current moment, but I think you're going to have to take your top off."

Ugh! I groan. I try not to put too much thought into the way he said 'at the current moment.'

"This isn't exactly how I pictured being shirtless in front of you. This is too embarrassing. Just leave me here."

He laughs. "I'm not going to leave you here. You're under the water. No one on the beach will be able to see anything. If it makes you feel better, I will try my hardest not to look." He has that ornery grin again.

"Fine. Can you untie me, please?" I point to the back of my neck while trying to hold on to the coral so I don't rip my top off completely. He swims behind me; his fingers gently untie the top knot giving me a second to hold the top against my chest. He places a kiss where the knot was, sending chills to untouched areas of my body. He undoes the second knot, again placing a kiss against my spine, causing me to shiver. He swims back in front of me, giving me a look. I know what he's going to say.

"You have to let go of the top."

Ugh. I slide my hand under the material and cover my breasts with one arm, letting go of the coral with the other. I swim sideways to give him room to work on unhooking my top. He sinks his face mask just under the surface to view what he is doing under the water, grabbing the bulk of the material in one hand and using his other hand to wiggle the material around. After several long minutes, he finally frees it. He hands my top back to me. Now comes the hard part: putting it back on without flashing the entire beach and without drowning.

"My hero," I tell him sarcastically.

"You're welcome." He laughs.

I swim around him so I can face out to sea with my back to Ethan and the beach, gaining some kind of privacy to be able to slip my top back on. I drop my arm from my breasts and tie the lower straps around my ribs. When I am done I work on the top straps but my hair keeps getting in the way. I feel Ethan behind me, gathering my hair, and holding it up as if it were in a ponytail. I blush wondering if he can see my chest from this angle. I quickly tie the strings and he places a kiss on the back of my neck before letting my hair fall. I spin around to face him.

"I think I am done with the water for today," I tell him, embarrassed.

"All right, let's get back up to the beach."

We hang out on the sand long enough for the sun to dry us off before we get into his Jeep.

"It's almost four. I need to go home and prepare dinner for my dad. Is it all right if I drop you back at yours then maybe we can go to a movie later tonight?" he asks awkwardly.

"Of course. I think it's noble you help take care of your dad," I tell him.

"You'd be the first. Anyone I've ever brought home has broken up with me a week later. Guess they didn't want to be with someone who has a handicapped parent," he says, withdrawn.

"That's shit. I think it makes you that much more of a man," I say, hoping it makes him feel better.

He smiles and leans over giving me a sweet quick kiss.

"I'll be back around eight. The drive-in is showing *Dirty Dancing* if that would be something you're interested in. I guess I should have asked if you even like that movie. I assumed all girls do. But you might be different."

"I am different than other girls in a lot of ways. My love for *Dirty Dancing* is not one of them." I laugh. *Dirty Dancing* is a classic; it's one of my favorites.

He smiles. "I'll see you at eight p.m. then."

I lean through the window, giving him a chaste kiss on the cheek. I walk up the drive, noticing my family's rental car is gone. *Great! I have the house to myself!* I am going to blast my music, take a shower, I might even walk through the house naked. Hopefully, they stay out until Ethan comes back.

57

Chapter 8

I strip my swimsuit off, taking a relaxing hot shower. It feels great on my sore muscles. I blast some *Beach Boys* from the shower stereo system since no one is home. I love listening to music while I shower but am never able to when my family is around. Some sand washes out of my hair and I notice the little cut on my side from where the coral caught me earlier. I take my time, steaming up the bathroom. When I am done, I rub lotion over my entire body, wanting to be soft and cuddly for the drive-in tonight. Since it is not too humid today, I decide to straighten my hair, leaving it down. I think I will lay out in the sun for a while beside the pool since I still have some time until Ethan arrives. I stretch out on my belly on one of the lounge chairs directly in the sun. Maybe I will tan a little. I have an alarm set on my phone so I have plenty of time to do my makeup. The sun is warm and a breeze is wafting the fresh scent of flowers through the air. It is so calm and relaxing that I can't help dozing off.

I wake up startled by my alarm, not realizing I had been asleep this whole time. I press myself up in a yoga pose flinching when I feel it. My entire backside is sunburned. I hadn't meant to fall asleep. I have been lying in the sun unprotected for almost two hours. I walk into my bathroom to check out the damage. Sunburn covers my neck, the entirety of my back, and down the back of my legs. My cheek is slightly burnt from my head being turned as I slept. Great. At least my front is unburnt. I can apply some extra concealer to help with my face. As for the rest, I will need to buy some aloe vera.

I do a heavy coat of concealer on my entire face, some eyeliner, heavy mascara and finish my look with some red lipstick. I slip into a black wavy mini skirt and a sparkly pink tank top hoping it will camouflage some of the red of the sunburn. It's uncomfortably rubbing on my skin but I'm going to have to suck it up. I hear the Jeep pull in, so I grab my bag and head out the door. Ethan is in the process of getting out of the vehicle when I walk out. He is wearing a simple grey t-shirt and a nice pair of dark blue jeans. There are designs on his butt pockets that really draw attention to that area.

"Thank you," I say when he opens my door.

"You got some sun," he jokes, seeing my back as I climb in. So much for camouflaging it. I was hoping he wouldn't notice so easily.

Once he gets in behind the wheel, I confess. "I wanted to lay in the sun for a while but I fell asleep. An hour and a half later, now I am a lobster. How did dinner go with your dad?" I ask.

He seems surprised that I asked. "It went well. I made his favorite fish tacos."

"Sounds yummy. Can we stop somewhere to get movie candy? It's my favorite part."

He smiles. "Of course."

We drive to the nearest convenience store, getting a front-row parking spot. I head straight for the candy aisle. Ethan seems nervous all of a sudden, he's looking around wide-eyed like he's going to rob the place. He's fidgety even.

"You okay?" I ask, wondering what is going on with him.

"Yeah. I'm fine," he says. "Can you grab me some Swedish Fish? I'll be right back."

"Okay," I say, trying to down play the awkwardness, hoping

I didn't do something.

I continue to peruse the candy, struggling to figure out what I may feel like snacking on. I like to get one chocolate and one fruity candy when I go to a movie. I grab his Swedish Fish, then settle on Raisinettes and Sour Patch Kids for myself. He hurriedly strolls back into the candy aisle.

"Is everything okay?" I ask again.

"Yeah. Everything is fine," he tells me, seemingly more relaxed, so I let it go. "Anything else you need?" he asks sweetly.

Embarrassed, I mumble, "Aloe."

He laughs and walks me to the pharmacy aisle where the aloe is located in the burn creams.

"Here, try this one." He chooses some Hawaiian-made peppermint, eucalyptus, aloe gel and hands me a bottle. "It takes away all of the pain and smells great."

"Cool," I say, taking it with me to the register.

The guy behind the counter smiles at Ethan in an odd way. Like he knows something I don't. He scans my items but Ethan hands him his card. "What are you doing?" I raise my voice more than I meant to.

"I am buying this."

"I guess I'll buy popcorn. Thank you," I tell him, sticking out my tongue. I tell the clerk thank you, but he just says, "Have fun, kids," directing it toward Ethan with a smile on his face. Ethan carries the bag to the Jeep and puts it behind his seat.

*

When we pull into the drive-in, there is a person in a purple floral Hawaiian shirt standing at the gate.

$5 PER VEHICLE—it says on a big chalkboard sign.

"That'll be $5," the worker tells us. I pull out my wallet, having cash on me.

"Here." I hand the five-dollar bill to Ethan. He looks skeptical about taking it but I give him a glare that lets him know I'm serious. He hands over the money and the guy raises the gate.

"Enjoy the movie!" he tells us. Everyone in Hawaii is so full of *aloha*. It's more than just a saying or a greeting, it's a way of life. It's an unmatched kindness.

We park in the back row since the Jeep is considered an 'SUV and will block the view of the smaller cars' according to the women directing traffic. Ethan opens up the tailgate revealing a couple of blankets and a bunch of pillows. I put down the back seats, grabbing the bag from the convenience store. I open the bag looking to grab the chocolate covered raisins but I notice a small black and gold box at the bottom of the bag. I pull it out to find a small pack of condoms. *Oh. This must be why Ethan disappeared at the store and why he insisted on paying. How did he sneak it into the bag without me noticing?* The clerk! That's why he made those comments to Ethan. He must have been the one who slipped them in the bag. Ethan is busy arranging the pillows in the back so he doesn't know what I've found. I walk over in front of him, bag in one hand, condoms in the other, holding them up while raising my eyebrows at him in amusement. This is going to be good. He looks up from the pillows, the color draining from his face when he notices what I have.

"I can explain," he blurts out.

"So, this is what you were up to at the store," I tease.

"I am so sorry. I'm not trying to... I wasn't... I didn't mean..."

He is stuttering and I am loving it. I can't hold back my smug smile at catching him with something embarrassing. Oh, how the tides have turned.

"I am not expecting anything, I just wanted to make sure we had something, in case something did happen. I'm not saying anything was going to happen, but I figured it was best to be on the safe side. In case you did want to. But if you don't, that's okay. You must think I'm a *pua'a'* now," he says, defeated, sitting down on the edge of the back compartment, running his hands over his face. It's sad to see him like this. I give up my teasing and sit beside him.

"You're cute when you stutter." He looks at me confused.

"You're not mad?" he asks cautiously.

"No. I finally have something to tease you with now," I tell him.

His shoulders relax. The movie starts so we situate ourselves in all the pillows getting comfy. I pull all of the candy out of the bag handing him his. I set the aloe aside, excited to put some on later.

"Sour Patch Kids and chocolate-covered raisins are an interesting combination," he quirks.

"You don't eat them together." I laugh. "You got to have one fruity candy and one chocolate candy for a movie. I never know which one I will feel like eating so I get one of each."

"You're nerdy. I like it. My favorite has always been Swedish Fish," he informs me.

I attempt to settle into the pillows, but I fidget trying to get comfortable. My back is burning with the friction against it. I want to put some aloe on but I don't want to be awkward and gross in front of him.

"Take your shirt off," he tells me straight up. He leans over me, grabbing the bottle of Hawaiian aloe.

"No, it's okay. You don't have to. I'll put some on when I get home."

"How are you going to reach your own back?" he asks, knowing the answer already.

"Okay," I huff, knowing I need the relief. I move to sit between his open legs. I hear the bottle open so I pull my shirt up on top of my shoulders.

"This is going to be cold," he warns. I jump a little as his hand touches me. The gel is cold like he said, but it instantly takes the sting away. He spreads it over my back, massaging my shoulders a bit.

"Is this okay?" he asks in my silence.

"*Mmhmm,*" I mumble with a nod. Too content to speak. He finishes by blowing on my back to dry the gel, then he gently pulls my shirt down. "You're right. That stuff is magic." I can't feel any of the burn I felt before.

"We Hawaiians make good shit." He laughs.

"I know your parents did an amazing job making you," I tell him with a smirk.

I am still sitting between his legs. Instead of moving, I lay back against his chest. "Is this all right?" I ask hearing him take a deep breath.

"Absolutely," he responds wrapping his arms around my middle. We watch contently, snacking on popcorn and Sour Patch Kids. We sneak in questions and little conversations. When the movie is over, we are slow to move away from our cuddle. It feels natural, like we've cuddled a thousand times before. I could fall asleep against his chest without a care in the world. As the cars fight over who gets out the exit first, I sit in Ethan's arms, drawing circles against his skin, making the tiny hairs on his arm stand up. I'm the first one to move away from our embrace as I

63

notice we are one of only three cars left. The irrational fear of one of the workers coming over to the Jeep thinking something steamy is happening and kicking us out sets in, so I fold the blankets while Ethan stacks the pillows.

"I had a really nice time tonight." I smile at him as we drive out the exit.

"I did too. You are an amazing cuddler." He smiles, entwining our fingers over the center console. He seems relaxed, happy. It's nice to think I can make someone happy for a change.

I don't know if it's the elated feelings I'm experiencing, or the urge to be young and carefree, or maybe even from being turned on from the sex scene in the movie, but something inside of me is saying to pounce on Ethan, right here, right now. It's telling me to go for it and not think about the consequences. I notice a dark pull-off on the side of the road up ahead that has no streetlights and currently no audience. I point to it asking Ethan to pull over.

"Is everything all right?" he asks, turning his hazard lights on.

Before I lose my courage, I unbuckle my seat belt and lift the armrest, allowing me to crawl across the bench seat. I slip my leg over Ethan's lap, catching him off guard. I grab his neck gently with my hands, bringing his lips to mine. His whole body stiffens for a second before he responds enthusiastically, placing his hands carefully against my back, pressing my chest into his.

I trace his lips with my tongue, making him open his mouth. Massaging my tongue against his, he lets out a deep groan. My fingers make their way into his hair, tugging his head back, exposing his neck to my mouth. As I lick from his collarbone up to his earlobe, he whispers, "Fuck," sending chills down my spine. I attack his neck with kisses, licks, and little nibbles.

Needing more skin, I grab the bottom of his t-shirt, pulling it up. He catches on, so he grabs the neck line and pulls his shirt the rest of the way off. I press him back into the seat so I can get a good look at him. You can see six abs chiseled into his abdomen, and he has a small white mark on his rib cage. I wonder what caused this little scar, but now is not the time to ask. I can't resist leaning down to pull one of his nipples between my teeth.

"Fuck!" he curses, thrusting up against the apex of my thighs, accidently honking the horn in the process. I take that as a sign I did something right. I switch to the other nipple and do the same, soothing the bite with a swipe of my tongue. His fingers are tangled in my hair, pulling my face back to his. His fingers play with the hem of my tank top. Leaning back I stare into his eyes as I pull my tank top over my head, revealing a dark pink pushup bra. In the darkness, I place his hands over my breasts physically giving him permission to do whatever he wants with my body to take some of this ache away.

He looks like I just made an unspoken wish come true. He's much more confident in touching me now that he has my permission. He pulls me close, running his lips over my neck like I did his. I can feel my insides clench. My hands are all over him, tracing his abs, scratching my nails over his nipples. He pulls my bra strap down, kissing the skin beneath. His kisses set me on fire. His mouth moves over the tops of my breasts, slipping his fingers under the material, preparing to pull it down to capture my nipple with his mouth.

There is a loud knock on the glass of the driver's side window. I scream, collapsing into Ethan's chest. "Shit" I hear him say. I look over and there is a cop standing there with a flashlight peering into the Jeep. He motions for us to roll the window down. I am frozen, having been caught shirtless on the side of the road, straddling Ethan's lap, so Ethan is the one who hits the window button on the door.

"Well, well, well, what do we have here?" the cop jokes playfully.

"Oh, God," Ethan states, hitting his head on the headrest behind him. He runs his hand over his face, trying to clear the make-out haze.

"Now, I know you can afford to get a hotel for the pretty lady, Ethan." I blush at being called pretty in my current lack of clothing. *Wait, how does he know Ethan?* I give Ethan a look and he sighs.

"Zoey, this is Charlie. Uncle Charlie, this is Zoey," he introduces us. *Another uncle! Seriously?*

"Nice to meet you, Zoey."

"Nice to meet you as well, sir. I'm sorry, this was my idea, please don't give Ethan a ticket," I beg, apologetically.

Charlie laughs. "I'm not giving him a ticket, but you two got to move this necking elsewhere. I pulled over because I thought something was wrong when I noticed Ethan's Jeep with the hazard lights on. He's the only person in Kauai with a neon orange *yota*. But nothing appears to be wrong, so I'm going to get on my way. Son, she is too sweet to be getting it on with you on the side of the road. Treat her with some respect and get a room next time," he directs at Ethan. Ethan looks like he's about to die but nods anyway. Charlie goes to walk off but Ethan stops him.

"Please don't mention this to Mom," Ethan begs of Charlie.

"Don't worry, kid, your secret is safe with me." He laughs as he walks away.

I look at Ethan for an explanation. "I don't want my mom to think this is the type of man I am. They raised me to be a

66

gentleman. Not some sex-crazed animal who takes innocent girls on the side of the road."

I wholeheartedly smile at him. "You are a true gentleman," I tell him, placing a sexy kiss on his mouth. I climb back to my seat, grabbing my shirt off the floorboards. We drive back to my place. My family still isn't home. Wonder what they are up to. We sit in the Jeep, processing what happened.

"Was that okay back there? I know it caught you off guard and then your uncle showed up. I guess I should have asked if you even wanted to kiss me. Are you mad at me?" I ask hesitantly, afraid I may have crossed a line.

"I am mad. That my uncle showed up, interrupting my removal of your bra." He smirks. "It is always okay if you want to straddle me and make out any time. We just have to find a more secluded spot next time." He winks. I laugh, at ease with his answer.

"So, what do you got going on tomorrow?" I ask him.

He smiles. "I unfortunately have to work. I got three tours to lead. I am covering the last one for Liam so he can leave early." I'm saddened, but I understand.

"Okay. I may go into town and do some shopping," I inform him. I lean back in my seat, enjoying these last few minutes with him. His hand is warm in mine resting on the armrest. He talks about a few local shops for me to visit tomorrow which I appreciate. I have no clue where to begin.

"Okay. Time for me to go. You need to get some sleep for work," I say.

He leans over kissing me, reigniting the fire from earlier.

"Thank you for taking the blame with my uncle; he's still convinced it was my idea but I appreciate the help." I laugh.

"You're welcome. Goodnight."

"Goodnight, Zoey," he says so gently, exhaling the words out of his mouth.

I climb out, sulking up the drive. watching him drive away, then head to my room. Since I'm not very tired, I lay in bed and watch a movie on Netflix. I hear my family come home but it's after eleven p.m. now, so I stay where I'm at, feigning sleep. When the movie is over I set my phone on the charger, rolling over. I can't wait until I see Ethan again.

Chapter 9

I wake up to Denise banging around in the kitchen. I sigh, walking out in my pajamas to see what's going on.

"What the hell are you doing?" I grumble, rubbing the sleep from my eyes.

"Mom and Dad went to breakfast by themselves, so I am stuck making something myself. Can you believe that?" I would want to leave her home too if Denise were my daughter.

"Move, I'll make it," I say, pushing my way through her mess to grab a skillet. She huffs but takes a seat at the counter. I mix up some eggs, adding spinach, cream cheese, and a pinch of sea salt. While they fry in the pan, I put some bread in the toaster. I give the eggs a stir as the toast pops up. I spread some butter over it, letting it melt, then I sprinkle some cinnamon and sugar on top. I pile some eggs on her plate with a couple pieces of toast. I put more bread in the toaster to make some for myself, then help myself to a scoop of eggs.

"This is actually good," she says. I know she meant it to be insulting but I take it as a compliment. She devours her plate before I am halfway through mine. I try to make some small talk with her hoping it doesn't bite me in the ass.

"So, what are you going to do today?" I ask.

"I don't know yet. What are you doing? Disappearing with that Ethan guy I suppose?"

"No, he has to work today. I was going to go into town and do some shopping," I tell her.

"Oh, shopping! I love shopping! I'll go with you!" she squeals, like I invited her. Before I can protest, she runs off to get ready. Great. My shopping trip just got hijacked.

Twenty minutes later, I'm dressed and ready to go. I call out to Denise that she better hurry if she wants to leave with me. Just as I give up on waiting for her, she skips out, overly dressed, swimming in some expensive perfume. "I'm ready!" she states.

We walk out of the house and down the sidewalk. She complains the whole way about having to walk, but I tell her it's better for the environment and not that far. She wants to get a coffee first since she claims that it is too early. We go into this small local coffee shop where we are greeted by a Hawaiian lady in a floral shirt behind the counter. "*Aloha!*" she greets us. Denise ignores her, starting her order. She orders some mocha soy triple pump caramel concoction that sounds disgusting. When it's my turn I greet the lady, asking about her morning so far.

We talk story, which means small talk, while she works on our drinks. I ordered the chocolate coconut macadamia nut frappe, which is ready first, causing Denise to get grumpy. I know the lady did it because I was nice to her. The first sip is like heaven. It's cold, creamy, and absolutely wonderful. Denise and I pay separately. The lady put a twenty-five percent *kama'aina'* discount on mine making it quite a bit cheaper than Denise's drink. I keep that between me and the lady though seeing as how Denise has already walked away and is waiting on the sidewalk. I put a $5 in the tip jar with a *mahalo* as I exit. Denise gripes about the poor service she received and how she won't be going back there. I sip my drink letting her words go in one ear and out the other.

"Let's check this place out," I say to Denise, grabbing the door handle of a clothing store. She walks in front of me, letting me hold the door open for her. "You're welcome," I say more to myself.

The store is full of young women's clothing. From skirts and dresses to shoes and belts. It's a cute little boutique. Denise squeals running off into the swimsuits. I make my way through the t-shirts and into the dresses. I end up in the lingerie section by accident. There must be fifty different styles of lingerie. Not to mention the regular panties and bras hanging on the walls. I look around, making sure Denise is nowhere near, as I stroll between the lingerie racks. I've never looked at this type of stuff before and I know she would make fun of me if she saw me. There are pink baby dolls and black lace body suits. All a bit much for the virgin I am currently. I come across a red lace bra and panty set. The bottom is a lace thong, the bra piece is padded the way I like, covered in a dark red lace. The dark and light red combination would pop against my freshly tanned skin. I grab one in my size and slip it between the other outfits I plan to try on, then make my way to the changing room.

I start with the black dress I picked up. It makes me look like a skunk with a white strip going down the middle. It immediately enters the no pile. Next, I try on this teal Kauai shirt that has a steep cleavage cut down the chest. *This one is a yes.* The skirt I got shows my ass but doesn't zip all the way, so I put it in the maybe pile if I can find the right size. Then I got this red dress. It is similar to the lingerie in the way that it is lacey. It is strapless and rides high on my thighs but it covers everything. I think of Ethan and what his thoughts would be on this dress. I put it in the yes pile. The last thing I have to try on is the lingerie set. It fits me perfectly. My breasts fill the cups, my ass looks amazing with just the small red strap disappearing between my cheeks. As I am checking myself out in the mirror, a hard pound on the door

71

makes me damn near pee myself.

"Zoey, are you in this one?" she yells. *Ugh, seriously? Right now?*

"Yeah, one second."

"No, open the door now."

Thinking it might actually be an emergency I crack the door, using it to cover myself. She is holding two pairs of flip-flops. "Which ones?" she asks seriously. I should have known it wasn't a real emergency.

"Holy shit!" she screams, looking behind me. I turn to look only to realize she could see what I was wearing in the mirror behind me. She pushes on the door, letting herself into my changing room. The door shuts, her jaw dropping as she stands there facing me. I try to hide using my arms but it's not helping.

"Is this for him?" she asks.

"I was just trying it on. It's not a big deal. I'm not getting it," I say quietly, turning to grab the clothes I was wearing. She grabs my shoulder.

"Yes, you are! You're not getting dressed yet. You need to take a picture," she says excitedly.

"What? Absolutely not!" I tell her.

"Oh yeah. Send it to Ethan. You look hot!"

"Uh, thanks. But no!" This is weird. She has never complimented me before. I'm not sure what to do.

"Give me your phone. I'll take the picture," she says.

"I'm not sure about this."

"Come on. What's the worst that can happen? He gets a boner at work?"

She has a point. I am trying to be more spontaneous.

"Okay." I hand over my phone. She takes pictures from all sorts of angles. She positions me standing in front of the mirror then she steps off to the side, making sure she is not in the picture. She angles the camera down as I stare into the lens.

"That's it! That picture is the one to send!" she exclaims loudly.

She tilts the phone to show me the picture she took. I am staring into the lens with my lips parted. My breasts stand out against the bold red but what catches my attention is that you can also see my ass in the mirror showing off the red lace disappearing into my crack. I have to admit, it's a sexy picture. Not sure I want to send it to Ethan though.

"Thank you, but I don't think I can send that to Ethan."

"Already done," she smirks, handing my phone back. I feel the life leave my body. I should have known better than to trust Denise. I snatch my phone back, noticing she has my text messages to Ethan open, and sure enough, she sent the picture.

"Why would you do that?" I screech.

"I was trying to help you get a boyfriend. You can thank me later," she says casually, slipping out of my changing room.

Oh my God. I think I might actually die. The message hasn't been read yet but there is no way to take it back now. *How do I explain this to him?* He's never going to speak to me again. He'll think I'm some creepy tourist just after sex with him. Alone in the changing room, I quickly get dressed, and grab the yes pile before walking to the checkout counter. He hasn't responded.

I pay for the clothes and the woman puts them in a purple sparkle boutique bag with the store logo on it. I need to eat before I pass out, so we stop for lunch. It's been seven minutes since she texted Ethan. Not receiving a response yet has my stomach turning. *Maybe he hates it or thinks that I am teasing him.*

"Earth to Zoey!" Denise says. I was zoned out, looking at the menu.

73

"Sorry. He hasn't responded," I tell her, giving away what I was thinking about.

"Well, you said he was at work. Maybe he's busy. Give him some time. If he doesn't respond then drop him," she tells me harshly.

When the server comes over, Denise orders a Caesar salad with a light dressing. Feeling like something light myself, I order the same thing. We make small chitchat over the salads, this being the first time we have gotten along, ever. My phone dings. I jump, grabbing it. Denise claps. "See?"

A single text from Ethan. Oh My God, it says. I smile, hoping that is a good thing. I don't respond, not knowing what to say back to him. After we're finished eating and the server brings our bill, Denise buys my lunch. "Thank you," I tell her.

"If you tell anyone I was nice to you, I'll deny it," she says harshly. Back to her normal self.

"Why are you being nice to me?" I asked, needing to know her motives.

"Because you let me tag along with you shopping even though I know you didn't want me to. I appreciate you not leaving me behind like my parents."

We walk through the rest of the shops. Denise buys souvenirs for all of her friends. I don't have anyone to buy for, which starts to make me sad. I am done with shopping, so once Denise pays for all of her stuff, we start walking back to the house. We put our swimsuits on and hang out in the pool for the rest of the afternoon. Samson even joined us for a bit, it was a pretty chill day. Around dinner, I order Chinese for all of us. Aunt Susan and Uncle Dan have yet to return. We lounge in the living room, watching some alien movie on the flatscreen, eating our Chinese. It's about eight p.m. when my phone vibrates.

I am outside, Ethan texted. My heart sinks. *What is he doing here?* I tell my cousins goodnight, sneaking out to the garage. I see Ethan standing there but I don't see his Jeep.

"What are you doing here? Where is your Jeep?" I ask, keeping my voice low.

"I parked down the street. Can I come in?"

"Denise and Samson are watching a movie in the living room so you have to stay quiet. Come on, we'll go in through my room," I tell him, motioning for him to follow me around the side of the house to the garden entrance of my room. My stomach is full of butterflies at the thought of sneaking a boy into my bedroom.

I take him around the house climbing over a bush to get to my bedroom door. Thankfully, I left it unlocked. When we are both inside and the door is closed, Ethan presses me into the wall, kissing me with a passion I have only ever seen in movies. His hands press into my back holding me to him. I am instantly responsive to him, pressing my hands into his sides until he winces. I pull away from the kiss.

"Are you okay?" I ask looking at his side, as if I can see the problem through his shirt.

"You almost got me killed today. Jeremy saw it."

"What?" I ask, not following.

"I was on the trails when I got your picture. We had stopped at a rest point when I checked my phone. I tripped over a tree stump, into a ditch. Jeremy jumped down to help me but he picked up my phone. He looked at the screen and said he would've fallen in a ditch too. I busted my side, so it's kind of sore," he tells me the story. I feel so bad. *He got hurt because of me. Or really, Denise.*

"I am so sorry. Denise sent that picture. I would never have been that confident. I was just trying it on when she barged into my changing room and insisted that I take a picture. I had planned to delete it later but she sent it to you before giving my phone back." I hide my face in my hands, tears welling in my eyes. He pulls them away.

"No need to apologize for looking so goddamn sexy and sending me a picture." His voice is deep, husky, full of desire.

"Can I see your side?" I ask, guiding him back so he can sit on my bed. He pulls his shirt up, revealing a large red patch, spreading across four or five ribs. The edges are already turning purple. "Oh, man. That is going to bruise badly," I say full of guilt.

"It was worth it." He smiles mischievously.

"So, you're not mad?" I ask shyly.

"Of course not. Did you buy it?" He raises his eyebrow at me.

My face heats up and by the smile on his face I know he knows.

"You did," he says, seeming happy. "I can't wait to see it in person."

To cover my blush, I climb in his lap and bury my head against his neck. I press my lips against his pulse point, earning a small gasp.

"Do you have to work tomorrow?" I whisper.

"No. I'm off. I have to make dinner for Dad around five but other than that I am yours if you'll have me."

"Yes, please. I was planning to get a tattoo if you don't mind tagging along."

"Sure. What kind of tattoo are you getting?"

"My mom and I were supposed to get matching turtle tattoos on my eighteenth birthday. I already have the design but I might

76

get two turtles to represent hers that she should have gotten with me," I tell him.

"Wait, is tomorrow your birthday?" he asks, alarmed.

"Yeah." I blush.

"Why didn't you say anything?" he asks.

"No one has celebrated my birthday in years. My family doesn't even acknowledge it. I've lost the joy in celebrating it."

"Well, we are getting that joy back."

"No, you don't have to. It's really no big deal," I tell him.

"Eighteen is a big deal. Please? Can I celebrate it with you?" He gently places me on the bed as he stands to leave.

"I have to go make some arrangements. I will pick you up at nine in the morning," he tells me.

"You don't have to."

"Shhh... I am celebrating your birthday whether you like it or not. But I hope you like it," he says giving me a quick kiss on my lips.

"Okay. I'll see you in the morning," I tell him, watching him sneak around the outside of the house.

Around midnight I walk to the kitchen to get a drink of water. I sit out on the patio until midnight hits and I whisper "Happy Birthday" to myself. I jump as the sliding door opens, revealing my uncle in his pajamas, carrying something in his hand. He takes a seat beside me, sliding me an envelope. My mom's handwriting is on the front *'To Zoey, on her eighteenth birthday.'*

"What is this?" I ask my uncle, tears brimming my eyes as I recognize the writing.

"Your parents had talked about bringing you to Hawaii on your eighteenth birthday. I found this in their safe after they died. I'm sorry they couldn't be here today but I wanted you to know that this trip was actually planned for you. I just let your aunt believe it was for our anniversary. Happy birthday, kid." My uncle gets up from his chair and walks back inside. Tears are pouring down my face. I open the envelope, it's full of $100 bills but there is also a letter.

To our one-of-a-kind daughter, happy birthday. If you are reading this letter, that means something has happened to me and your father. We put this letter aside, knowing we tend to be a bit wild and reckless. We are sorry we cannot be there for your birthday. Inside this envelope is $18,000. We want you to use it to live your life. Get outside of your books, travel the world, fall in love. Do something crazy with it. We talked to Dan about Hawaii to ensure you made it there. I will write a contact below to our best friends who live in Kauai. Contact them, please. They would love to see you. Maybe they can even help you cope with our loss. We love you. We are watching over you from above, I promise we won't let anything happen to you, so please live. Happy birthday darling. Love Mom and Dad.

Keone and April Kealoha.

Phone number: 808-445-9867

Address: 405 Queen Avenue, Waimea, Kauai, Hawaii 96796

My eyes have turned into storm clouds and my tears are rain. I came to Kauai with only $2,000 that took me the past six months to save up. Now I've just been handed enough money to go to school or get my own apartment. Uncle Dan arranged this whole trip for my birthday. I am in shock by that. This whole time I thought he, like the rest of them, hated me. I wish I could talk to my mom. Any time I would be crying, no matter the reason, she would lay my head in her lap and play with my hair as I explained the situation. I could really use her comforting hands in my hair right now. I go back to my bedroom, placing the note and money carefully on my bedside table. I crawl in clutching a pillow to my chest and let myself cry every tear out of my body. Eventually, when I've run dry and covered my bed in tissues, I fall asleep.

Chapter 10

It's rough waking up when my alarm goes off at eight a.m. I'm groggy and feel dehydrated from all of my crying. I don't even need to look in the mirror to know that my face is swollen. I know I have to get up and prepare to celebrate this day with Ethan but I really wish I could just rejoin my dreams.

It's my birthday. My eighteenth birthday. A guy I really like wants to celebrate it. I need to try to enjoy today. I stand in the shower letting the water wash away the dried tears. Looking into the mirror, my eyes are swollen and red. I sneak into Denise's bathroom to borrow some of her under-eye cream to mask the puffiness. It does little to help my situation. Once I am covered to the best of my ability with my makeup and having added some red glittery eye shadow, I dress in the red dress I bought with Denise, concealing the red lingerie underneath it. Tonight might be the night for me and Ethan. I wear some matching red flip-flops and my mom's necklace. Today is going to be a good day, I try to convince myself.

Since it's early, Ethan texts me that he is here instead of knocking. I slip out the garage door to his Jeep. He is standing there in a white button-down and khaki shorts. He looks so tan and handsome. The spikey-styled hair drives me crazy with lust. He is holding a blueberry muffin with a pink candle on the top. He lights the candle when he sees me.

"Happy birthday," he says excitedly. He looks tired, making me wonder how long he was up last night.

"Thank you." I smile as I blow out the candle. My excitement for the day starts to arrive with his presence. He opens my door and then hands me a coffee. The same one from in town yesterday. I mentioned to him how much I loved it but I didn't think he would remember.

"Chocolate coconut macadamia nut frappe," he tells me placing the blended beverage in my hand.

"Thank you so much," I say, falling head over heels for this guy.

"Do you want to talk about whatever happened last night?" he asks, not wanting to make me feel pain but wanting to know why I've been crying.

"What do you mean?" I ask, trying to avoid this conversation so I don't cry anymore.

"I can tell that you've been crying," he says, placing his hand in mine, offering his support.

I pull the letter out from my bag, handing it to him to read.

"Are you sure you want me to read this? It seems kind of personal," he asks.

"Yeah, it's from my parents. I guess they left a letter prepared in case one of their outings killed them. And apparently, I am here in Kauai because of some arrangement they had with Uncle Dan. This whole trip is secretly for my birthday." I give him a minute to read the note, watching his eyes skim the page. When he gets to the bottom, his body becomes rigid and his face pales.

"Zoey?"

"What?"

"Keone and April Kealoha? Those are my parents. That's my address." He meets my eyes.

"What the hell?" I whisper, looking at the letter.

"It's okay. We will figure this out tonight. I had planned to surprise you with dinner at my place," he says, springing into action.

"That sounds nice," I tell him, climbing into the Jeep, elated that he seems to have a plan. I switch his radio on, searching through the channels, trying to take my mind off of the new information I've discovered.

"Where are we going?" I ask as he drives us away.

"It is a surprise." He smiles mischievously, not taking his eyes off the road. I play with his hand as we drive to the other side of the island, guessing off possibilities just to get no response from him. We off-road a little bit on an unknown trail. He parks the Jeep under a palm tree off to the side of an open field. There is nothing but grass in this mile long clearing.

"Um. Ethan?" I question, reminiscing the feeling of that first day when he disappeared with me into the woods.

"Just give it a minute."

All of a sudden I hear a whooshing noise. Leaves start flying around us as the grass blows in waves though the clearing. It's hard to see anything sitting under this tree. I open my door to get out and that's when I catch sight of it. A black helicopter—coming in for a landing—setting down softly on the grass. My eyes are wide as I whip my head around to question Ethan. He's got a cocky grin on his face.

"Helicopter ride. Check!" He makes a checkmark in the air with his finger.

"Are you serious?" I yell over the whirl of the rotators.

"I have a friend who flies helicopters for a tourist company," he tells me.

Ethan grabs my hand and we take off running to the helicopter. I follow Ethan's lead when he ducks to avoid having his head severed by the rotors. He opens the door and helps me in. There is a guy in a black polo wearing headphones with a mic in front of his mouth. Once Ethan gets in, the guy moves the mic to the side and turns to us.

"Ethan! *Howzit?*"

"Not bad, *braddah*, celebrating this girl's birthday today. Thanks for doing this for me," Ethan says.

"Not a problem. Anything for you, man."

"Zoey, this is my buddy, Keloni. Keloni, this is Zoey," Ethan introduces us.

"Nice to meet you!" I yell over the noise. He stretches his arm out to shake my hand.

"You two buckle in. Put a headset on. Enjoy your ride and thank you for flying Hell's Helicopters," mocking his spiel from work. I do as he says and buckle myself in extra tight. I am thrilled but scared all at the same time. I am in a freaking helicopter! I can't believe Ethan would arrange this. I watch out the window as Keloni lifts us into the air. He goes slow at first but once we are up into the air, he throws the bird forward, causing my stomach to lurch. I am bubbly with the feeling. We fly over the ocean looking out for miles. We can see the other islands of Hawaii. Keloni slows it down and points out the right window. As I look, I see what he was pointing at. Three humpback whales breaching the surface. I watch as water sprays from their blowholes. I've never seen a whale up close like this. It feels magical. I could sit here all day watching them glide through the water. We fly away heading to circle over the island. We pass over the beach where I learned to surf, I can even spot the drive-in movie theater. It's peaceful up here. I could stay up here permanently if that were possible. It's quiet and my thoughts have slowed. We fly for at least two hours, until I lose track of time, admiring all of the fascinating aspects of life on Kauai.

"It's time to head back guys. What did you think, birthday girl?"

"I don't ever want to land," I say over the mic.

"I never do either but until they make a heilo with an endless supply of fuel, we always have to come back down. Though just for a little bit in my line of work. I'm up in the air, probably eight or nine hours a day." I'm jealous. I would love to fly around all day, showing this volcanic creation to travelers.

When we land back in the field, I am reluctant to unbuckle. Ethan grabs my hand and smiles at my sadness.

"We can do this again another time but we still have a lot more birthday to celebrate."

I smile and climb out. "Thank you so much!" I yell back to Keloni.

"Anytime, *sissta. Aloha*!" With a *shaka*, he sends the bird straight up in the air, much faster than he did with us inside. Ethan holds my hand as he walks us over to his Jeep. As he reaches for the handle, I press him into the door. He looks at me bemused.

"What are you doing?" he asks playfully.

"Saying thank you for a fucking awesome birthday." I close my mouth over his before any more words can come out. I run my hands up his chest and into his hair pulling him down to me. His hands run down my back, very slowly over my ass, really holding on before he moves his hand lower to catch behind my knee pulling it up to his hip. He moves his hand back to my ass squeezing my cheek over my dress. I am getting lost in his kiss. He slips his hand under the hem of my dress moving up my thigh. He cups my ass cheek in his palm, but his mouth stops moving against mine. I pull back to look at him. His eyes are dark, like

84

he wants to throw me on the hood and unleash himself onto me.

"What it is?" I ask, breathless, ignoring the fact that I said those words backward, wondering why Ethan stopped.

"Are you not wearing panties?" he asks making me turn a shade of crimson. I should have realized when he put his hand under my dress, there wasn't much covering anything down there. Score one for the red lingerie. Instead of answering him, I place my hand over his, still on my butt, sliding it even higher until his fingers fumble over the strap of the thong.

"Shit," he groans closing his eyes, attempting to regain his composure. Driven by teenage hormones, adrenaline and pure happiness, I lean forward pressing the tip of my tongue against his pulse point, tracing it up his neck to whisper in his ear, "I can show you if you'd like?" I ask in a soft voice. He nods but keeps still. I pull away and open the passenger side door, hopping up in my seat, pulling my dress up around my hips. When Ethan looks at me I spread my legs, watching as his gaze drops to my center. He licks his lips, contemplating his next move. I want him between my legs. The hormones coursing through my veins masking any sense of self-consciousness. Ethan drops to his knees outside the door. Face level with my core. He strokes his hands up my legs, holding my knees, as if he's afraid I am going to close them, never to open them for him again.

"Can I…?" he stumbles, asking for permission. He can have permission to do whatever he wants to me right now as long as he takes away the ache. He kisses my thighs, working his way up the left side to kiss down the right side. He kisses his way back up, making me tremble, pausing to look at me for any sign of opposition, then moves his mouth to my center. My breath catches at the feeling. His tongue slides over my pussy, straight through my lips, over my clit, making me whimper. I lean back against the armrest as I struggle to breathe. His hands hold my thighs open as he licks me up and down. I feel like passing out when his tongue presses inside me. His name slips from my mouth as I slide my fingers into his hair, giving a slight tug.

"*Ahhh...*" He's circling his tongue around my clit, making me feel like combusting.

"Ethan!" I call out his name over and over, hoping he realizes what he is doing to me. *Fuck!* He is so good with his tongue, knowing exactly where I want it. He slips his tongue inside of me again, using his thumb to rub my clit. That's all it takes to send me over the edge.

"I'm coming!" I scream into the empty field. My vision glazes over in stars and fireworks instead of seeing the trees and sky. He keeps licking, sucking, rubbing until I am overly sensitive and twitching against the seat. With one last lick up the center, he pulls his head away. I look down to see his lips glistening in my arousal. It's the most erotic thing I have ever seen. His tongue slides over his lips, collecting every drop of me, as his eyes bore into mine. I rush forward, sealing my mouth over his, tasting a sweetness with a tangy metallic aftertaste. It is absolutely delicious as I suck myself off his lips. I want more. I want him right here, right now.

"Zoey," he whispers in a hoarse voice, breaking the kiss. *Mmm* is all I can manage.

"Not here. Not right now. I don't want your first time to be in this field, against the side of my Jeep." I know he's right but it feels like rejection. Maybe he doesn't want me.

"No, none of that. I can see what you're thinking and that is not the case."

I look into his eyes as he rests his forehead against mine.

"Zoey, I promise this will happen. I will make love to you. I will make you scream my name until it's the only one you can remember, but not in this field. Not in the Jeep. I want to make it special."

"God, why do you have to be so perfect?" I whisper, stealing another kiss from him.

He stands up, stepping back when I notice the front of his shorts. He has a wet stain surrounding his zipper. I flush thinking of him coming as he ate me out.

"Did you…?" I eye him, pointing my finger toward the stain.

"Yeah, I did," he states, face turning red from embarrassment. "I couldn't help it, the way you reacted to me, pulling my hair, moaning my name. Orgasming on my tongue made me explode. You taste so sweet. The way your back arched in my face. When I looked up seeing your face as you orgasmed, I lost it." He walks to the back of the vehicle and pulls a fresh pair of jean shorts out of a duffel bag.

"Shit. I didn't grab any boxers. Guess I'll be going commando for a while." I situate myself in my seat, pulling my dress down and buckling in, trying to give him privacy as he changes behind me. It's about noon and my stomach growls.

"Is lunch included in today's adventure?" I quirk, hinting at the lack of lunch in our first one.

"Of course. Anywhere you want. I just had my lunch," he winks, catching me watching him in the rearview mirror. I blush, turning back around.

"I feel like… The Lobster Hole! I want to try their salmon," I tell him about the entrée Samson had on our first night here.

"You can have whatever you want today."

I want you, I say under my breath so he doesn't hear me. Once he is dressed, he climbs behind the wheel, staring the engine. We drive to The Lobster Hole. We ask for a table outside sitting closest to the water away from people. I am looking over the desserts when our waitress walks up.

"What can I get you two to drink?" she asks politely.

I look up, asking for a virgin piña colada.

"Hey! You're the girl from the other day. I remember you. The girl at your table kept throwing a fit over her steak," she tells me. Her name is Amanda.

"Oh yeah! Sorry about that. My cousin can be a brat," I say remembering her.

"Oh, I've put up with worse. I'll be right back with your drinks," Amanda tells us.

Ethan ordered a virgin strawberry daiquiri. I am set on the salmon while Ethan chooses shrimp kabobs. Gross.

Amanda comes back carrying two very fancy beverages, with whipped cream and a cherry on top. Ethan has a strawberry on the rim while I have a slice of pineapple. Yummy!

"Oh my God, those look fantastic."

"They are amazing. What did you guys decide on for lunch?"

"I will have the salmon and he has decided to eat the yucky shrimp." Amanda laughs at my childish objection to his choice.

"All right, I'll get that sent back to the kitchen." She walks away and I notice Ethan smiling at me.

"You're cute," he tells me playfully.

"What?" I ask, unknowingly.

"You act like a five-year-old at the thought of shrimp but you had your legs wrapped around my neck thirty minutes ago." That makes me blush. He sips his straw sexily, flicking his tongue like he did on my clit. I look out over the water to avoid his gaze. There are dozens of sailboats of all colors and names. I even spot a wrecked sailboat against the shore, that I must have missed the other day. Some of the boat names are inappropriately hilarious: Test Tackles, Ship Happens, Master Baiter. My dad would have got a kick out of these boats.

"So, where to next?" I ask, curious.

"You have a tattoo appointment," he tells me.

"You made me an appointment to get my tattoo?" I am touched he would do such a thing.

"Yep. As soon as we are done here. I wanted you to eat something before."

"Thank you." I feel so cared for, something I haven't felt in years.

Amanda comes back, dropping off our food. "Here you go. One salmon, and one icky shrimp." She laughs setting our plates down.

"I've got to go to the bathroom, I'll be back," Ethan states, hurriedly walking after the waitress.

I squirt lemon juice over the top of the salmon, it smells delightful, with garlic butter dripping over the sides. When I take a bite it melts in my mouth like ice cream. It tastes so fresh, so much better than the salmon at work. Ours is frozen and shipped from Alaska. This right here is fresh, probably caught off one of these boats, and seared to perfection. Ethan comes back, plucking a shrimp off his plate with his fingers, popping it in his mouth. We eat a little quicker, knowing we have an appointment to get to. As I am taking my last bite of juicy salmon, Amanda comes from behind me with some kind of chocolate dessert with a sparkler on top of it. Ethan must have told her it was my birthday.

"Happy birthday!" She sets the dessert down in front of me. "Make a wish!"

I make a wish then blow on the sparkler knowing damn well that thing will have to burn out on its own. When the sparkler dies, I carefully pull it out of the top, setting it on my empty plate. Amanda picks up the dirty dishes and walks away, wishing me a happy birthday one more time. I give Ethan a look, letting him know, that I know what he did. He gives me that prized grin of his. The dessert is like a chocolate mousse with cake underneath, there are blueberries and strawberries on top, with chocolate shavings sprinkled all over. It is almost too pretty to eat. I pull my phone out to take a picture before I dive in with my spoon.

"Oh my God. This is delicious," I moan savoring this chocolate heaven in front of me.

"*Ono*. Means delicious in Hawaii," Ethan tells me.

Amanda drops off the check and I hand her my card as Ethan is pulling out his wallet.

"I am buying this." I look at him sternly. "You have bought almost everything else. I get to buy this one."

"But it's your birthday," he argues.

"But nothing. I want to buy you lunch today." I end the discussion.

Amanda brings back the tip slip for me to sign. She wishes me a happy birthday and then goes off to take care of a new customer who just sat down. I leave a fifty percent tip knowing it will make her day. And it makes me feel good to make someone else happy. Ethan watches me take the last bite of chocolate and lick my spoon clean. I consider licking the bowl but that would be inappropriate in such a fancy restaurant so I put it down. I get up, reaching to take his hand in mine so we can head to the Jeep.

"We can actually walk to the tattoo shop from here. It's right up the road."

"Oh, is it that one in town here?" Denise and I passed it the other day while shopping. He gives me a nod. We walk for about ten minutes then he grabs the door to the tattoo parlor. I walk in, looking around, at all the art covering the walls. Different tattoo designs from three different artists who share this place. The wall is a mural painting of the ocean with three surfers riding a wave. Whoever painted it has some wicked talent. A guy in a black shirt with tattoos for sleeves comes walking out from a closed room with a girl who looks uncomfortable. It appears to be an awkward situation. The girl keeps her head down with her arms across her chest as she hurries out the door.

"Nipple piercing. She got offended that I wouldn't fuck her on the table. Just because I pierce tits doesn't mean I want to fuck everyone who shows them to me," the guy gruffs.

Ethan walks over to shake his hand. "Hey, man."

"Sup cuz? Who's this?" the guy asks.

"Zach, this is Zoey. Zoey, Zach."

"Nice to meet you. I promise I won't try to sleep with you for doing my tattoo." I laugh, hinting at the last girl.

He smiles. "I would appreciate that. My husband would kill me for becoming a pussy lover."

"So, what brings you guys in today?" Zach asks.

"It's her birthday," he tells him. Apparently, he has to tell that to everyone we encounter.

"*Hau'oli la hanau*. What can I tattoo for you?"

"I want a small turtle on my wrist," I say simply not feeling like bringing down the mood with the sad details. I've decided to just get the one turtle, not wanting to be reminded every time I look at it that Mom isn't here.

"I can do a turtle. How do you want it? Tribal, traditional? Any colors?"

I look over the designs on the wall before answering. "Can we do tribal with some red swirled into the shell?" I ask.

"Nada problem. Follow me." He leads us into a private room

similar to the one he walked out of earlier but this room has a chair like a dentist's office to recline in. I sit down while Ethan pulls the extra chair out of the corner and sits to my left side. Zach is busy printing off the stencil while I fidget in the chair.

"Which wrist?" Zach asks and I hand him my right. He places the stencil on, pressing into my wrist firmly, transferring the design. When he pulls the paper away there is a blue tribal turtle left in its place. I admire the little design, excited to make it permanent. Zach puts the armrest of the chair down and lays my arm, wrist up. He pulls up his tray of needles, ink, and paper towels.

"Ready?" he asks.

"Let's do it," I respond with enthusiasm.

The needles, covered in black ink, puncture my skin and a warm burning sensation fills the area. I thought it would hurt a lot worse than this though. I watch as the stencil changes from blue to black, becoming permanent. It takes Zach about fifteen minutes to do the entire turtle in black. Next comes in the red swirls. I bleed a little as the needles pump the red ink into the turtle shell. *I wish Mom were here.*

"She's watching you right now," Ethan speaks quietly, having been silently watching me this whole time. *How is he always able to read my mind?* "Your mom would be so proud of you." I smile. He understands and accepts me for who I am and what lies in my past. I squeeze his hand.

"*Pau*," Zach says finishing the red, doing his final wipe. He smears some goo on the irritated flesh then puts a small square of saniderm over it.

"The wrap should start peeling off in about five days. Wash it twice a day after that; don't submerge it in any water. Put a light coat on after washing. You're all set," he says, handing me a small tube of the tattoo goo. We walk up front where the register is so I can pay.

"$55," he tells me.

I hand him $70. "Keep the change." He smiles. "*Mahalo*. You have a great day celebrating your birthday, babe. Ethan? Bonfire on Friday, ya?"

"Shit, I forgot," Ethan responds, looking conflicted. He looks at me. "Would you want to go to a bonfire with me?"

"I'd love to."

"Looks like we will be there," Ethan says to Zach.

"Great. See you then," Zach says as we walk out the exit. My wrist is stinging but I smile at it as we walk back to the Jeep.

"Are you happy?" Ethan asks sincerely.

"I am more than happy."

When we get inside his Jeep, we sit there in silence for a few minutes. It's serene. It's about three p.m. now. I wonder what is next on the agenda.

"So, where to next?" I ask, unable to wait.

"My place," he says. That catches me off guard. "I'm making dinner for you. And it gives you the chance to meet my parents and figure out the letter."

"Are you sure?" I ask, anxiety flaring. I know this is what needs to happen but I'm nervous. I have wanted nothing more than to talk to his parents since reading that letter last night.

"Of course. We need to figure out the connection they have to your parents." I squeeze his hand hard out of nervousness as he begins the drive to his home.

Chapter 11

Ethan pulls into the driveway of a beautiful family home. It's painted green with a two-car garage attached to the side, white shutters and window frames, with a red Chevy Malibu sitting in the drive. I also notice a destroyed motorcycle, leaning up against the side of the garage, the one from the accident I assume. The flower bed is full of color, with bees swarming around, collecting pollen. Not only am I meeting my boyfriend's parents, if boyfriend is what he is, but I am meeting longtime friends of my parents that I knew nothing about until yesterday. I am scared. *What if they don't like me?* Before a thousand more 'what ifs' pop into my head, Ethan grasps my hand, kissing my knuckles.

"I've got you. No matter what. If at any point this is too much, just say the word and I'll take you back to your house."

"I'm good," I say, faking confidence.

We walk in the front door, being met with the welcoming smell of a burning candle. There is a hallway going to the right but if you go left, you walk into the open layout of a living room on the left-hand side and a dining room area to the right. You can walk straight and there appear to be three other rooms. Once you go through the dining room, there is the kitchen to the right with the candle I smelled, burning on the center island. Everything looks so homey and inviting. A real family lives here. It's not all white and metallic like an operating room, like the cold house I've lived in for the past three years. The living room has dark brown carpet, a flat screen TV on the wall, with a movie shelf underneath lined with classics such as *St. Elmo's Fire* and *The Breakfast Club*. I wonder who the movie fan is. I am standing beside the kitchen island when a tall, dark-haired woman walks out of one of the closed doors at the end of the hall. She is walking with her head down but looks up upon entering the kitchen. When her gaze flicks over to me, she drops the tray of dishes she was carrying, glass shattering everywhere, and she collapses into the dining chair beside her.

"Mom!" Ethan yells rushing to her side.

"*Dear Pele*. It's like seeing a ghost," the woman whispers, as Ethan crouches next to her.

"Mom, this is…" Ethan starts to introduce me, but his mom interrupts him.

"Zoey Martin. Daughter of Anna and Doug Martin." His mother breathes as if all the air has left her lungs.

"Hi. It's nice to meet you. I'm sorry to surprise you like this."

"Oh no, dear, I'll be fine," she tells me.

"How did you know my parents?" I ask as she regains her composure.

"Honey, can you pour us some pog. We have a lot to talk about."

"Sure, Mom." Ethan stands, moving to the refrigerator to pull out a pitcher of pog. I have learned that pog is passionfruit, orange, and guava juice. It's really tasty. He pours three large glasses, bringing them to the dinner table.

"Come. Sit." The woman motions me over to have a seat. She has a broom in hand, sweeping the broken glass into a pile to be picked up later.

"First off, I'm April. It's so nice to see you again, dear. I haven't seen you since you were about three. Today is your birthday if I remember correctly, right?"

I am shocked that she knows this information, and that she had known me as a toddler.

"Yes, it is." Keeping my response short.

"Well, happy birthday, dear. I wish your parents could see this. Their daughter sitting here with me in my kitchen on her birthday."

"How did you know them?" I ask again. April smiles, sensing my impatience, and gets straight to the point.

"Your mom and I were best friends. We met in college and instantly hit it off. We never went anywhere without each other. We even went on each other's honeymoons. Your dad and Keone became really close friends. You guys lived here in Kauai until you were three years old, then you moved to Michigan to help out your uncle. He was struggling with a gambling problem, about to lose everything, when your dad stepped in to help him straighten out his life." April gets up and walks over to the mantle under the flatscreen, grabbing a picture frame I hadn't noticed before.

"Here." It was a picture of Mom and Dad holding me, standing beside April holding Ethan and who I assume is his father, standing next to her. I gasp. I've seen this picture before. I grab my rucksack, hanging on the chair I am sitting in. I tear through the interior looking for the photo album. My fingers run across its spine, quickly withdrawing it. I flip through the pictures until I find the same one April just handed me. I lay it open on the table.

"That's us. We were celebrating Keone's birthday at the beach. You two were just babies." She smiles at the memory. I've seen this picture a hundred times and never put much thought into the strangers I was staring at.

"Wait, Ethan, when is your birthday?"

"December 6, 1999," April speaks first. "He was due in February but arrived early. He was in the NICU for ten weeks, with a tube in his chest, until his lungs were formed enough for him to be able to breathe on his own. The doctors didn't think he would make it, but I knew my little man was strong," she says, sounding immensely proud of Ethan. I smile at him noticing him blushing at his mother's praise.

"Your mom and I were trying to get pregnant at the same time, so you guys could grow up being friends, but it took your mom a little longer to conceive. Still, there was only going to be a six-month difference but that turned into eight months. You two did everything together up until the day you left. Ethan cried, hugging you, refusing to let you go with your parents. He was upset for two months afterward. It's remarkable seeing you two here together. How did you find each other?"

I look over to Ethan. "My family came here on vacation. I met Ethan on the ATV tour at Piku Ranch. My Aunt didn't want me to go so she sabotaged the reservation for only four people. Ethan had me ride with him when he overheard."

"That's sweet. Your aunt always was a mean one. Your mom was always complaining about how someone could be so selfish. I am glad Ethan was there to save your trip."

I smile thinking of my mom hating Aunt Susan equally as much as I do. Ethan stands up, and walking over to the fridge, he pulls out a few items, setting them on the counter. "I am going to get started on dinner."

"Okay, honey, what are we having tonight?" his mom asks sweetly.

"Well, since it is Zoey's birthday, I am making my parmesan crusted chicken with rice and a tossed salad."

"Oh yum. That sounds delicious," I tell him, mouth already watering.

"I hope you'll like it." He smiles back, turning his attention to the stove.

"So my parents lived here?" I return to my conversation with April.

"Yes, they moved out here when they were eighteen. They were on a school trip but fell in love with the island, so they transferred and got an apartment. Your mom wanted to be a nurse, that's where I met her. We had the exact same class schedule, spent most of our time in and out of class together, studying, surfing, going out to eat. I met Keone a year later, and we became a four-pack. We were inseparable. Two years after graduation, I found out I was pregnant with Ethan and a couple months later your mom found out about you. We were in each other's delivery rooms. I watched you come into this world. The day after you were born, Doug walked into the hospital room with the key to the house he bought for Anna. He and Keone had built this little pink nursery that sent your mom into waterworks when she saw it. She loved the house. She was always working on the flower beds or doing something to add more color. Your dad even made her an art room for all of her paintings. Your mom and I were together every day with you babies while our men went to work, we would take you guys to the beach or to get a snow cone. We had a lot of picnics. Ethan was very fond of you. Always being your protector. I remember once, you were barely walking and a wave knocked you over. Ethan shouted at the wave calling it a *lolo* then dragged you out of the water. Your mom and I were laughing so hard."

I look over at Ethan, but he is turned toward the stove, working on his chicken. I think I see a smile on his cheek though.

When I face April, I see her smiling at her son.

"She had the best laugh. Not a day goes by that I don't miss her laugh." She did have the best laugh. I miss her so much. A tear slips down my cheek, and April passes me a tissue.

"Dan got into some trouble with gambling, Susan was about to take the kids and leave. He called your dad, begging for his help. As much as Doug hated to leave, he knew he needed to help his brother. So your parents moved back to Michigan; they would still come to visit from time to time but they never brought you with them. They always bragged about how much you loved your school work and that you were going to be an amazing doctor."

I am full-blown crying right now. "Can I use your bathroom?" I plead.

April looks sorrowful as she points down the opposite hall. I hurry to close the bathroom door, pressing my back against its cool surface. Tears pour down my face. I gave up so many opportunities to spend time with my parents and now they're gone. I'll never get that chance again and this pain is too much to bear. I am such a mess, sobbing in Ethan's bathroom. After what feels like forever, there is a light tap on the door.

"Zoey, can I come in?" Ethan asks. I don't want him to see me like this.

"I don't want you to see me crying," I whisper hoarsely.

He opens the door slowly, walking in with his eyes closed. "I don't want to disrespect your wishes, but I can't let you cry alone, so I promise to keep my eyes closed." He never looks at me, just shuts the door behind him and then collects me in his arms. I start sobbing against his chest. He lets me cry, soaking his shirt with my tears, completely falling apart in front of him. I start to run out of tears, struggling to catch my breath, hiccupping as I inhale. He smooths his hand over my hair, telling me that it's okay and that he's here. Eventually, I calm down, drooping in his embrace.

"I'm sorry," I tell him sadly.

"There's no need to apologize."

"It's really hard to hear all of this stuff about them. I never knew any of it."

"I know. Do you want to leave?" he asks, wanting me to be comfortable.

"No. I'm okay. It's good to hear. Just hard," I tell him, regaining my composure.

"I'll give you a minute, then meet me back in the kitchen, yeah?"

"Thank you, Ethan." I say, grateful for the moment to fix my make-up and not look like a total mess on my birthday. I pee, then wash my hands checking out the damage to my face. A few sparkles have run away with my tears and I'm blotchy red, but the rest of my make-up looks intact. Hopefully, once I cool off, the redness will go away. I take a deep breath, then exit the bathroom. His mom looks up at me and stands. I see she has been crying too.

"Honey, I'm so sorry, I upset you."

"No, it's all right. I am sorry. It's overwhelming to find out all this new information about them without being able to talk to them about any of it."

"I understand. Come here." She pulls me into a hug. It feels nice to have a motherly figure hugging me, comforting me. It makes me miss my mom even more.

"Dinner is ready," Ethan says from the stove.

"Oh good. I'll go get Keone. He was taking a nap," April says, walking out of the kitchen into one of the bedrooms. I walk over to Ethan checking out his chicken in the pan.

"That looks amazing," I tell him, eyeing the saucy, cheesy chicken. "Can I help with anything?"

"Nope. Just sit your cute butt back down in your chair," he says leaning over to give me a quick peck on my lips.

I'm sitting at the table when April comes out of the bedroom pushing a wheelchair.

"Holy fuck," comes from the man in the wheelchair.

"Keone!" April hisses, smacking his arm.

"I apologize. You look just like your mother. I'm Keone."

I give him a smile. "It's nice to meet you, sir."

April positions him on the side of the table that has no chairs. She grabs some plates and silverware, setting the table. I offer to help but get turned down again. Ethan carries over the pan of chicken, setting it in the middle of the table. He grabs the bowl of salad off the kitchen island. When the oven beeps, he pulls out a pan of breadsticks that I never saw him put in. He even puts them in a fancy warming basket.

"Woah, Ethan, this looks outstanding," I tell him in awe of this tasty-looking food.

He blushes with the compliment. "Nice work, son. What's the special occasion? You save your chicken recipe for important events," his dad states.

Ethan looks embarrassed. So, he made a special dish just for my birthday. I smile at him giving him an eye of amusement.

"It's Zoey's birthday," Ethan tells his dad.

"Of course, it is! *Hau'oli la hanau*, darling!" Keone cheers happily.

"Thank you. It's the first one I have celebrated in years. Ethan is going all out."

"That would explain the p—" Ethan shoots his dad a glare that says stop talking. "Never mind."

We sit around the table like a family. I couldn't tell you the last time I had a homestyle meal like this. Ethan piles my plate full of food, I can see the uncertainty on his face, unsure if I will like his special chicken. As soon as I take a bite, I know this is my favorite meal. It is creamy, with garlic, cheese, and breadcrumbs. He grated fresh parmesan on top, same with the salad, which has tomatoes, spinach, feta, with some sort of oil drizzled on top. I watch as he tosses the salad and then serves some to everyone. The breadsticks are fresh and so soft, maybe from a local bakery, unless he made them himself too.

"This is the most *ono* meal I have ever eaten!" I announce to the table, using my newly learned Hawaiian vocabulary. Ethan looks happy hearing that. "I'm glad you like it."

"Where did you get this bread from? It's so soft and fluffy. I could eat this every day of my life."

"It should be good. Ethan was up at five a.m. rolling out the dough." Keone lets me know.

Ethan looks down, embarrassed his dad just ratted him out.

"You made the bread? At five a.m.? For me?" I ask stunned. *Why would he go through that much trouble for me?*

"Well, yeah. I wanted you to have an amazing day," he replies, making eye contact with me.

"Thank you. It has been wonderful." I hope he understands how much today means to me. He has done everything to make today a good day. I appreciate his effort, it's nice to feel special.

The rest of the meal is eaten while Ethan's mom and dad relive the past, sharing stories of my parents. I listen as April and Keone recount memory after memory. There is so much laughter around this dinner table. I ask questions, they answer, and vice versa. They ask about my life when my parents were still alive and how I am doing now. They both seem to have a hatred for my aunt. This is the best birthday present anyone could ever give me. When we are done eating, Ethan clears the plates away, placing four small plates down on the table. I look at him curiously as he gets something from the fridge. He comes back to the table with a coconut cream pie, recently learning it is my favorite.

"I am guessing you made this yourself too?" I asked, already knowing the answer.

"Sure did. Swatted my hand with a spoon when I tried to steal a piece this morning," Keone says.

I already love his dad. He's so open and honest about everything Ethan has been doing for me today. Clearly a proud parent. I can see Ethan is embarrassed, but I love hearing everything his dad has to say. Ethan presses two candles into the top of the pie making '18' then lights them with a match. He stares at me with a blinding smile, "*Hau'oli la Hanau!*" he tells me.

I blow out the candles as everyone claps. Ethan cuts us all a slice of pie, making mine bigger than the rest. I gaze at this yummy dessert covered in coconut shavings and merengue. I am in heaven. I eat every bite except the crust, fearing I will burst open like a piñata.

"Dinner was delicious honey," his mom informs him.

He says, "Thanks," bashfully walking out of the dining room into what I assume is his bedroom. In his absence, I gather up the empty dessert plates placing them in the sink. It's almost eight thirty p.m. Time flew by tonight. Ethan walks out, kissing his mom on the cheek.

"I will do the dishes when I get home."

"Okay, honey. You two have fun for the rest of the day. I am going to get your father into the tub," she tells him standing up, squeezing behind the wheelchair.

"It was nice to meet you, darling, but it is time for my sponge bath. The nurse is a doll, I'm hoping to get lucky tonight," Keone says.

"Keone! *Hush!*" April smacks him again, turning red in the face. I laugh. Ethan rubs his hand over his face at his dad's comment. April moves around to hug me.

"You are welcome here anytime, dear. We have a spare bedroom." I tear up at her sentiment.

"Thank you so much. I appreciate that," I say, hugging her.

His parents disappear into the bathroom, leaving me and Ethan alone in the kitchen.

"I love your parents," I tell him happily.

He smiles, brushing a strand of hair behind my ear. "Are you ready to go?"

"Where?" I ask, knowing he isn't going to tell me.

"It's a surprise," we say in unison as I mock him.

Chapter 12

Ethan drives us to Piku Ranch and parks beside the wooden cabin. He gets out, with me following close behind him.

"Are we breaking into your work?" I whisper, scared we're doing something we shouldn't be.

"It's not breaking in if I have a key," he whispers back, sarcastically. Of course, he has a key.

When we are inside the cabin, he walks behind the check-in desk, grabbing another set of keys.

"What are we doing?" I ask, still concerned we are going to get in trouble.

"I thought I would take you on a moonlit tour to the waterfall?" he says hesitantly, gauging my reaction carefully, I smile to let him know that I am all in.

We exit the cabin, Ethan locking the door behind us. He grabs his duffel bag from the Jeep then walks us over to the same green employee ATV he drove the day we met. I situate myself in my seat, lacking a helmet this time, since we're not on an official tour. He tosses the bag in the back then jumps in, staring the engine and turning on the headlights. We drive slowly through the woods; in case an animal runs out in front of us. I am kind of scared of the dark, honestly. Though I know I am safe with Ethan. He is my protector and apparently has been since birth. Pulling up to the waterfall, it is drenched in moonlight, with a full moon overhead, shining through the trees, illuminating the waterfall just like the sun did. Ethan grabs the duffel bag and my hand, walking down to the sandy part at the bottom. Ethan positions me so I am standing facing the falls.

"Don't look. Keep your eyes on the water," he tells me.

"What are we doing?" I laugh.

"Give me just a minute."

"Okay," I say excitedly. It seems important to him that I don't look, so I stay facing the water. The breeze gives me chicken skin as it gusts off of the water. I can see a flicker of orange light on the surface of the water, as well as a strong beam from what I am guessing is a flashlight. I'm nervous. *What is he doing behind me? What is this last birthday surprise going to be?*

"Okay, you can turn around," he informs me a few minutes later. I feel him standing beside my shoulder as I turn. Laying on the sand is a blanket surrounded by tea-light candles shaped into a heart. Pink flower petals are scattered, with a square, gold wrapper on the upper corner of the blanket. It looks like a scene straight out of a movie. It's so romantic!

"If you want to. But if you don't, we can just lay here and look at the stars," he says.

"You set all of this up for me?" I ask in shock at such a romantic gesture.

"I wanted your first time, our first time to be special. If you're not ready, we don't have to do anything," he tells me, peering into my eyes, looking for any sign of objection.

Placing my hands on his hips, I gaze up into his light brown, nervous eyes.

"Ethan. Make love to me. I want you to be my first," I tell him from the bottom of my heart. I don't care if we only have a few days left together, or that we might part ways, never to see each other again. If my parent's death has taught me anything, it's that tomorrow is not guaranteed. I want to experience

106

everything life has to offer, before my time comes, and who better to experience this with than Ethan.

He caresses my face between his palms, kissing me softly. It's sweet, tender, impassioned. He backs me up toward the blanket, only breaking the kiss to make sure I don't burn my foot on one of the candles. He guides me down to a red, polyester blanket in the middle of the candle heart, kissing lightly. I'm the one who deepens the kiss by swiping my tongue across his bottom lip, asking for entrance. He obliges, wrestling his tongue with mine, fighting for dominance. I let him win, I want him to dominate me. He presses me to lay back against the blanket, as he lays off to my side with his arm gently draped over my waist. He rubs his hand over my hip bone, against my rib cage, lingering on top of my breast as our kiss heats up, filling me with a fire-like desire. I grab the hem of his shirt pulling it up over his stomach until he sits up, pulling it off the rest of the way himself. I want to lay here admiring him on his knees, shirtless, but the dark blue and black bruise on his ribs contrasts against his olive skin making my heart stop. I bolt upright, clutching his waist.

"Ethan!" I panic. He looks down worried then realizes I'm staring at his bruise.

"I fell harder than I thought." He shrugs it off like it's no big deal. I get up on my knees examining the bruise. It's large, taking place of the reddish, purple mark he had there last night.

"I'm okay," he tells me, grasping my hands.

"I'm so sorry. You got hurt because of me."

He nods silently knowing what he wants to say but rethinking if he should.

"Consider it payback," he says softly, approaching the topic on his mind.

"What do you mean?" I ask, not understanding what he's

talking about.

"It's probably going to hurt tonight. I'm going to try to make it as painless as possible but, if you want to stop at any time, just tell me, and I'll stop," he says distressed by the thought of hurting me.

"Ethan, I know it's going to hurt. I trust you. My body is yours tonight," I whisper pulling him back against my lips. His hands slide up my back, pressing my covered chest into his bare one. My fingers rub over his pectoral muscles, dragging my nails across his nipples, knowing he likes that. His hands run down my backside stopping at the hem of my red dress.

"Can I take this off?" he asks, eyes still closed, blissed out from our kiss.

I nod, letting him pull the dress over my head, revealing the laced red bra, the sister piece to the thong, he saw earlier.

"*Nani 'oe.*" He exhales.

"You're overdressed." I point to his pants taking the attention off of myself. His gaze is making me fidget. He stands up kicking off his shoes, dropping his pants. I notice he's wearing boxers again after going commando this morning. That must have been what he went into his bedroom for. I lay back on the blanket pulling him down, over me, resuming our kiss, as he gets comfortable between my thighs. His kisses against my neck make my body feel like molten lava, flaming and liquid. I arch my back so he can slip his hands behind me to undo the bra. When it falls loose, I toss it in the sand away from us, watching as his eyes move to my chest. He catches on to my uncomfortableness at his stare, because he leans his head in, catching my nipple between his lips. I gasp, slipping my fingers into his hair. He circles his tongue around the hardening bud, sucking, then gently biting as he pulls away. He blows on it, watching it harden in the cool night air. He switches to the other side doing the same thing. I can feel the wetness pooling between my legs. He's got my body tingling, ready for him to take me away on this sensual journey.

"Ethan," I moan, "I need more."

"Are you ready already?" He pulls his head back to look in my eyes, questioning if I am really ready.

"Touch me," I urge him, guiding his hand between my legs. His fingers trace along the outside, teasing me, before moving my thong to the side and running up my slit. I moan at the feeling. His finger circles over my clit a couple of times, before descending deeper. He stops at my entrance, meeting my eyes as he gently pushes his finger into me. My breath catches as I let out a moan, I can feel myself clench around the intrusion. The feeling is indescribable.

"Do I turn you on this much?" he asks staring at his hand, as he pumps his finger in and out. I'm clinging to the edge, about to embarrass myself by climaxing on his hand.

"Ethan... I'm going to... if you don't stop..."

He watches my face as his finger slides back up to my clit, covered in my wetness, slipping around in circles. My body starts trembling as my legs attempt to close themselves but his arm is in the way. When he bites my nipple, closing his warm mouth around it, I'm done. I have one hand covering his on my clit, keeping him there and one in his hair, pressing his face into my breast. My walls clench, orgasmic release dripping out, eyes screwed shut as I spasm under him. He pulls away, boring into my soul through my eyes. My eyes dilate, watching as he brings his finger to his mouth, sucking it clean.

"*Ko aloha makamae e ipo,*" he whispers.

He sits back on his knees pulling his boxers down, tossing

them over the candles. He is bigger than I had imagined. As he pulls my thong off, he places my feet on his shoulders, pulling the material down my calves. He spreads my legs, gazing into my center as he lays back on top of me. I can feel his erection pulsing between us.

As he reaches for the condom, he stops, getting serious.

"Are you sure?" he asks, needing my permission.

"Yes Ethan, please." I need him in ways that I don't fully understand, to extinguish the fire burning through my being.

He nods, opening the wrapper with his teeth. He pulls out the condom, reaching between us, sheathing himself in the thin latex.

Slowly, he presses into me, watching my face for any sign of discomfort. The pain comes when he is about a third of the way in. It aches but I have a feeling it is about to get worse. His face is an open book, displaying all of his feelings.

"Ethan. It's all right. It's about to hurt a lot, you are really big, but just kiss me, okay?" I rub my hands over his back, trying to soothe him.

"I'm sorry," he mumbles against my lips before kissing me. He pushes deeper into me, breaking my hymen, causing an extreme burning sensation to fill my lower half. The stinging makes my eyes water, causing a single tear to slip down my cheek. I feel a drop of water hit my face from above, causing me to open my clenched eyes; I don't remember seeing any rain in the forecast. The droplet is from Ethan. His eyes are closed tightly but two tears have escaped. The one that landed on my cheek and one that is still resting on his own. I hold his face in my hands, wiping the tear away with my thumb. He is tearing himself apart for hurting me.

"I'm okay, Ethan," I whisper, watching his eyes pop open.

"Please don't hate me."

"I could never hate you," I tell him. "It's all right to move now."

"You are so fucking tight." His eyes are closed, barely holding onto the shreds of his sanity. He stays still, giving me time to adjust. My whole core throbs, but I feel so close to him. I never want him to leave my body. I scratch his back with my nails as he kisses my neck trying to soothe me. The pain doesn't disappear completely, but it definitely helps. As I start to relax, I give him the go-ahead to keep going.

He pulls out again, making me feel empty without him inside of me, my body is happy to welcome him back in with his next thrust. With each thrust the pain starts subsiding, pleasure consuming me. He slips his hand between us, thumbing my clit, while sucking on my neck. I don't care if he leaves a mark. He can leave as many marks as he wants.

"Shit. Zoey. I'm about to cum." Ethan sounds extinguished yet energized at the same time. His thumb swirls harder over my clit, pushing me over the edge. My walls clench around him, swallowing him inside me. I don't even have time to warn him before I reach my breaking point. He can feel it though, holding strong for a few more deep thrusts. He cries out my name into the empty night sky, then collapses on top of me, not bothering to hold his weight. I embrace him, stroking his hair, both of us sweaty and out of breath. This is a feeling I want to experience every day of my life.

"Are you okay?" he asks, lifting his head. I nod, unable to speak. Using his arms to hold himself, he presses up, moving to sit on his knees, slowly pulling out of me. Pain pulses between my thighs, a deep throbbing, feeling empty with his absence. I notice his eyes widen as he looks down.

"Uh, Zoey? You're bleeding," he says, trying not to startle me, when he sees the condom covered in blood.

"What?" I panic, raising up on my elbows, looking between my legs. I slide my fingers between my thighs, only to pull them back covered in crimson. Shit. "I'm sorry," I tell him, moving to stand up. I step over the candles, heading for the water, when my shaky legs give out, landing me on my knees in the sand.

"Zo!" Ethan yelps, moving over to me. He grabs my arms, holding onto me. "Hey, it's okay." I glance into his eyes, waiting for his disgust, for him to get up and leave.

"I don't want you to think I'm disgusting. All the boys on the soccer team used to complain about girls bleeding," I tell him, letting him in on my fear of him taking off.

"A boy might. But I'm a man," he states, holding my arms, helping me stand. He wraps his arm around my back, sweeping the other behind my legs, carrying me bridal style into the water. The cool water soothes my sore muscles, washing away the blood, Ethan nuzzles into my neck, holding me tight against his chest as we wade through the water.

"I am honored to be covered in your blood; you gave me your virginity. Me," he whispers against my neck. He sets me on my feet when we are waist-deep in the water, keeping my back against his chest.

"Spread your legs," he tells me.

I do as he says, feeling his hand between my legs, gently rubbing his fingers against me. He strokes me so slowly and tenderly, slipping his finger inside of me. He is washing away the blood and bodily fluids with his fingers in the most compassionate act I have ever experienced. There is nothing suggestive about this, just the tender cleansing, as he pumps his finger in and out of me, making my head fall back against his shoulder. When he is finished, he wraps both of his arms around my waist, holding me in the pool of moonlight. I tilt my head up, seeking a kiss, which he obliges, so soft and sweet, full of love and admiration.

*

When he pulls into the driveway of the rental house, he turns off the engine, looking over at me.

"Would it be okay if I stayed the night?" he asks nervously, as if I would say no.

"I would like that," I say brushing my fingers through his drooping hair.

"Okay." He smiles. "You head in, I'll park down the street, then meet you at your door."

"Okay," I say jumping out, excited that he is staying. I haven't had a sleepover since I was twelve, let alone with a boy. I sneak through the garage, opening the door to find the kitchen empty. Everyone must already be in bed. I head to my room, locking the door behind me before kicking off my sandals. A hot shower sounds delightful. I'm sticky and sore from the long day we've had. Maybe Ethan will want to join me. I am mentally freaking out when Ethan taps on the garden door, making me jump. I get up quickly to let him in.

"I think I am going to take a shower," I tell him heading into the bathroom, unzipping my dress. He looks saddened to have to sit here without me though I don't let him suffer long.

"You're welcome to join me if you want," I say as sexy as I can, closing the door behind me.

I am unlatching my bra as he slides in the door behind me. I turn around to face him, happy he decided to join me, noticing

113

his eyes wandering over my fully naked body in front of him. He clears his throat, moving to take off his shirt. It amazes me that someone like Ethan can get so tongue-tied by my body. I step into the glass shower turning the water fully on hot. I let it run over my sore muscles as Ethan steps in behind me.

"*Oh,* you like it hot. So do I," he says surprised at the water temperature. I pull him against me so we're both standing beneath the showerhead, wrapping my arms around his waist, laying my head against his chest. We stand like this for a while until I decide my next move. I step out of the spray, letting him soak his hair as I grab the shampoo. I pour some into my hand, motioning for him to turn around. The water pounds against his chest as I lather the shampoo through his hair. I scrape my nails against his scalp, catching a small shiver run down his body. After a few minutes, I turn him around to rinse his hair. I apply some conditioner then grab my loofah. I get it bubbly in my coconut body wash, circling it against Ethan's back. I pass the loofah over his buttocks and down his legs, when I stand back up, I tell him to turn. He is facing me, letting the warm water rinse away the bubbles on his backside. He watches my every movement as I start on his chest, working over his arms, sliding over his abs, taking a minute to press my finger into the scar that I now know is from his breathing tube in the NICU. I'm nervous for the next part, knowing I'm about to be on my knees in front of him. If I weren't so exhausted, I'd be down to return the oral favor. His eyes are wide as I lower myself to the floor of the shower, allowing me access to wash his lower half. He watches as I twirl the loofah over his hips and thighs. I scrub his calves, carefully saving his cock for last. I work back up his legs, settling on his growing erection. I carefully hold him in one hand as I wash him with the loofah in my other, his eyes are closed, pressing his hands into the wall of glass. I take my time washing

114

this area, squeezing him in my hand. By the time I am done, he has a full hard-on. He apologizes for his body's response, as I stand up, moving him back into the spray of the shower, letting it cascade over his chest. I kiss his chest as I smooth my hands over his body rinsing away the soap. He looks like he could fall asleep standing here. He steps to the side, letting me get the full force of water, allowing me to soak my hair, he reaches for my shampoo.

"Your turn," he says huskily.

Feeling his fingers massage my scalp sends chills down my spine. I back into him, feeling his erection against my ass, getting turned on again. He spins me around, letting the water rinse the lather from my hair. I can't resist the urge of wrapping my arms around his neck and kissing him deeply. He pulls back first.

"Eh. You're not done yet," he says grabbing my conditioner. I whine but turn around, leaning my head back for him. As he smooths the conditioner through my strands, I sneakily rub my butt against him, hoping to provoke him.

"Zoey," he growls.

"Yes?" I ask innocently.

"You are making it very hard to finish this shower."

I turn around, pressing my chest into his. "Sorry. Showering with you is really turning me on," I say, embarrassed.

"If I had brought a condom in here, I'd already have you pressed against this glass, but unfortunately they are in the bedroom, so if you want more, we have to finish this shower."

"Fine," I grumble.

He rubs my loofah over my body like I did his, spending extra time circling my breasts. He takes a knee in front of me to wash between my legs as he presses kisses into my hip bones. I feel his soap-covered fingers grab a handful of my rear. My body is heating up, not from the water, but in response to his

115

ministrations. He lifts my leg, allowing himself access to my feet, but also spreading my thighs in his face. My hand splays against the glass wall in an attempt to keep myself steady. Once he is done with my toes, he stands up, pressing me back into the spray from the shower head. I am quick to rinse, turning the water off and grabbing two fresh towels off the shelf. I dry myself, leaving my hair dripping as I pull Ethan into my bedroom.

My body can't delay another minute. He makes quick work of retrieving a condom from his bag, as I lay myself on top of the comforter, spreading my legs for him. He smiles, climbing over me on the bed, kissing my lips before sinking into me. I gasp at the intrusion, not feeling any of the pain from before, only pleasure. He bites my neck, soothing it with his tongue. My vision shatters into fireworks and glitter as I come around him, calling his name quietly, so as to not wake up the household. He continues thrusting through my orgasm, not giving my body a second to cool down. I feel like a live wire, pure electricity coursing through me. Surprisingly enough, I feel myself rising up again, preparing to explode in another orgasmic eruption. He thrusts harder, faster, whispering obscenities in my ear. As I reach my peak, he groans, emptying himself into the condom. His eyes meet mine as he stares at me in wonder. Placing a tender kiss against my mouth, he climbs off to dispose of the used latex.

When he comes back, he snuggles into the blankets I've climbed under, pulling me tight against his body.

"Ethan?" I ask, hoping he's still awake.

"Zoey?" he whispers back.

"Thank you for an absolutely perfect birthday," I tell him sincerely.

"You're welcome."

Snuggled into his warm embrace, I drift off to sleep.

Chapter 13

There is an alarm vibrating against the pillow. Groaning, I roll over, trying to find the source of the annoyance. Running my hand over a bare chest, I jolt awake, forgetting Ethan had stayed the night. As I come back to my senses, he is snoozing the alarm. He wraps his arms around my middle, pulling me tight against his chest, with his lips right above my ear.

"I have never wanted to call off so badly."

"You have to go to work though," I tell him, making him groan. I flip over so I am face-to-face with him.

"Good morning." I smile.

"Good morning," he replies. I press my mouth against his, meaning for it to be an innocent kiss but soon, I find myself deepening it, pressing my tongue against his. I caress his chest with my hand, moving lower, until I wrap my hand around him. The groan he lets out, encourages me to continue. I kiss my way down his neck, gently rolling him onto his back, following so I am on top, straddling his hips. I rub my wet center against him as I suck and nibble on his neck.

"Oh God," he moans beneath me. He grabs my hips flipping us so that he can be on top. He kisses me hard, fueled by desire. He captures my hands, pinning them above my head.

"What do you think you're doing?" he asks huskily.

"Making you late for work," I reply, wrapping my legs behind his back, keeping him against me.

"You're going to get me in trouble," he states, not seeming

bothered by the thought. He smiles, kissing me, but breaks it to slide over the edge of the bed, grabbing a condom out of his duffel bag.

I find it extremely sexy when he rips the condom wrapper with his teeth, like he did last night. He slips it between us, covering himself, then tosses the empty package on the nightstand. He kisses me softly, lining himself up with my entrance, pushing in slowly, in case I show any sign of pain. With one steady thrust, he submerges himself fully, meeting no resistance. I stretch, feeling my walls tighten around him. Everything feels so raw and tender. I love the way he gently strokes my hair, the way his teeth feel against my neck. I claw my nails across his back, spurring him on, sinking them into his ass cheeks.

"Fuck," he groans out, as I suck a spot on his chest, blood pooling to the surface, leaving a mark. When I pull his nipple between my teeth, he loses it, coming with a few deep thrusts. I don't orgasm this time, the overwhelming sensations taking my attention away but the feeling is amazing. It's so deep and strong and carnal. I want to do this every day, all day. With Ethan. It's like Bella and Edward in *Breaking Dawn*. How do you stop?

Once Ethan catches his breath, he pulls out, disposing of the condom in the waste basket beside the bed, sitting himself on the edge.

"I can't stop myself from coming with you. I used to last over an hour and now I blow in ten minutes."

"Is that good or bad?" I chuckle awkwardly.

"Good. Definitely good. Sex has never felt so good with anyone else," he tells me.

"Really?" I ask, feeling kind of special but not wanting to get my hopes up.

"Yeah. I haven't been with a lot of girls, but the four I have hooked up with were nothing like that." I smile, kissing his lips again.

Ethan rolls out of bed, standing with his cock perfectly at eye level with me. Just as I'm about to close my mouth on him, he walks around the bed to grab his duffel bag. Setting it on the bed, he pulls out a pair of socks, a clean pair of shorts, boxers and his tennis shoes.

"Shit," he mumbles under his breath.

"What's wrong?" I ask, worried.

"I don't have a work shirt with me. I could've sworn I put one in here. I'll have to wear the backup one that's in my locker."

"Or you could go shirtless all day. I don't see a problem with that," I say, winking at him.

"Oh, sure so all the girls can crash their ATVs? No, thank you. I'd prefer you to be the only one gawking at this shirtless bod."

"Shirtless, pantless, I'll gawk at any part of your body," I joke with him.

"Okay, babe, I've got to go. Rest up today. Maybe I can come back tonight," he winks.

"Yes, please," I say, getting a quick goodbye kiss.

Ethan exits through the garden door, leaving me to fall back to sleep for a few more hours. Waking up around eleven a.m. is way later than I ever sleep in. I rinse off in the shower before getting dressed to start my day. I gel my hair, already feeling the island humidity. There is a purple mark on my neck, catching sight of it after wiping the steam from the mirror. I know it's from Ethan; last night when he was sucking my neck, he left a hickey. I smile all the while blushing, alone in my bathroom, thinking about last night. He made my first time so special, even leaving

119

a memento for me to look at throughout the day.

I decide it's probably best to cover it up, as to not upset my aunt or uncle. Aunt Susan would probably scold me for being a whore and go off on a rant about abstinence. My foundation isn't doing much so I sneak to Denise's bathroom, knowing she'll have what I need to cover a hickey. When I open my door, I notice the house is empty. Everyone is outside, sitting around the pool. I haul ass to her bathroom, where there are dozens of products scattered on her sink. I pick a couple up reading the labels, trying to find the best concealer.

"Ahem! What are you doing in my bathroom?" Denises questions annoyed, walking in behind me.

I slap my hand over the hickey. "I was just looking at your makeup."

"Yeah, sure. What are you trying to hide? Pimple? Cold sore? Ah ha! You have a hickey!" she states proudly, figuring it out as she pulls my hand away from my neck.

"I just want to hide it from your parents. I don't need to hear it from Aunt Susan."

"If she knew half of the stuff I've done, she'd enroll me in an all-girls college. Here." She hands me a stick of what looks like lipstick but its skin tone. "This has always done the trick for me."

"Thank you," I say, grateful for her help.

I leave her bathroom when I hear her say, "You owe me." Great, just what I need, to be indebted to her.

After covering the mark on my neck and putting on my bathing suit, I head out to the pool with everyone else. Uncle Dan is taking a nap in the hammock, Denise is filming herself sitting poolside, while Samson has his nose buried in a book. Aunt Susan is lounging in a chair, soaking up the sun into her wrinkles.

"Oh, you're still alive I see," snarks my aunt.

I don't bother replying. While rubbing on some sunscreen, I sit on the side of the pool, introducing my skin to the temperature difference, before sinking down to swim some laps. I complete fifty laps before taking a break.

"Pizza's here!" Samson yells through the sliding glass door. He must have answered the doorbell when he got up to fetch his cell phone. My stomach growls. I'm hoping they got one with pineapple. Walking into the kitchen, everyone is filling their plates, I grab a slice of cheese and one of Hawaiian which has ham and pineapple, noticing Uncle Dan has that pizza on his plate too. It seems we have similar tastes. I take a seat at the end of the table, joining the rest for lunch.

"I have a surprise for everyone. We are going to a luau on Sunday night," my uncle states calmly, not looking up from his pizza.

"Oh, darling, how wonderful! Thank you!" my aunt starts.

"They only accept reservations for four or six people."

"Oh, honey, that's fine. Zoey will, of course, stay here. Or run off with that boy she has been hanging out with. I see he's already got you tatted up like a gang member. You better not bring him in this house while we are at the luau," she informs me hotly.

"I made the reservation for six. Zoey, you are welcome to bring Ethan," says my uncle, glancing at me while bracing for the explosion from my aunt.

"WHAT? She cannot bring that boy! She should stay here and let us have some family time."

"She is part of our family, like it or not. It's already paid for. Invite Ethan, Zoey. I am off for a round of golf. See you guys for dinner." He stands to leave, taking his unfinished slice of pizza with him.

"Wait! Am I not coming with you?" Aunt Susan shrieks.

"No, it's for men only. Sorry, honey. Next time, I promise." He waves leaving us all at the table, even my aunt. I can see the smoke beginning to pour from her ears.

"You little bitch! I don't know what has gotten into Dan's head, but you better not impede on our luau. Be nonexistent when we are there. And you and that boy will have to drive yourselves. There's no room in our car for sluts," my aunt tells me through her teeth.

"Don't worry, I won't make a scene," I tell her, scampering off to my bedroom. Her words hurt more than they should. I let the tears escape down the side of my face. I lay face down on my bed, taking a moment to collect myself. My phone vibrates, making my heart race, hoping it's Ethan.

Samson: "Would you like to walk into town for a snow cone?"

I am shocked. Why would he want to go with me to get a snow cone? He is probably going to ask me to skip the luau. But I feel like he would just come out and say that to my face. He's never had a problem hurting my feelings before. Maybe I should go to see what he wants.

"Sure." I type back, getting off of my bed. I open the door to see the living room empty, aside from Samson, who is still sitting at the dinner table, texting. Standing when he sees me exit my room, he holds his finger to his lips telling me to stay quiet. He opens the garage door, motioning me through. He doesn't speak until we are out of the driveway, walking on the sidewalk toward town.

"So, why did you invite me to get a snow cone?" I ask, cutting to the chase.

"My sister is the slutty one. Not you. I wanted you to know that my mom took it too far and that she was wrong."

"Oh. Um. Thanks. It means a lot to hear that."

"Mom has always hated you, your parents were outgoing and carefree and she hated them as well. When you first moved in with us, she felt like you were disrupting her picture-perfect family."

"Why are you telling me all of this now? You have never been nice to me."

"I feel it is time to grow up and move on. I mainly hated you to stay on my mom's good side but now that I am at college, I don't see much point in pretending anymore. Denise told me that the two of you went shopping. She actually seemed like she enjoyed it."

"I sort of enjoyed it too," I tell him because it was kind of nice having another girl to hang out with.

We arrive at the snow cone shop called Snow in Hawaii; I order a guava pineapple snow cone while Sam orders a lemon lime one. He even buys mine, which I thought was very kind of him. We take them outside, sitting on a bench to eat them. He seems kind of awkward as if he wants to talk about something but doesn't know how to start.

"Can I talk to you about something? You have to promise not to tell my mom," he asks me.

"I promise."

"I'm gay. I have a boyfriend. We've been together for six months. All summer, when I have been away doing research labs, that's just been a cover. I've been staying with him." He confesses.

"What's his name?" I ask, unsure how to handle this new information.

123

"Aiden. He is a chem major at Brown. We had a couple of classes together last semester."

"Does Denise know?" I ask.

"Yeah, she knows, only because she listened in on one of our conversations we had over the phone. I had to pay her not to tell Mom." Of course, he would.

"Well, you don't have to pay me. I think it's cool that you've found someone. Maybe one day you can bring him home to meet everyone."

"That's what I am afraid of. He wants to meet everyone, for me to finally come out to Mom."

"If he's willing to stand by your side and bear the explosion from your mother, then maybe you should consider standing up to her. It sounds like he's pretty serious about you. She should be happy as long as you are happy."

"You know she will break out her Bible, probably hit me with it in an attempt to turn me straight."

"If Aiden makes you happy and you want to be with him, then you need to take control of your life and stop letting Mommy control it for you," I tell him, irritated by the fear instilled by Aunt Susan. It's not just me, but her own son too.

"Ouch. But I get it. I do want him. Maybe when we get back, you could help me arrange a dinner or something," he says, nervous at the thought.

"Sure, I can do that. I'm happy for you."

"Thanks. I really like him," he says, smiling. "So, tell me about your Ethan. We have barely seen you since the ATV tour."

"He's kind. Ethan makes me feel alive, like the person I was before losing Mom and Dad."

"It's nice seeing you come back to life. I thought you had given up there for a while."

"I did, but I'm not anymore. Life is too short."

We talk for a long time about our boyfriends, his college courses, how crazy his mother is; we talk about my parents and their adventures, I tell him about Ethan's parents being close friends with mine and about the letter, his dad gave me. It's becoming easy talking to Sam, like we are close cousins, friends even. People who aren't having their first friendly conversation.

On our walk back to the beach house, he apologizes for being mean to me for all these years. I tell him that I understand, his mom can be influential at times but that I forgive him and hope we can be friends. When we get back, the car is still gone and the house is quiet. As we walk into the kitchen, Denise comes running out from the hall.

"Where the hell have you two been? I have been stuck here with Mom bawling her eyes out about how unfair her life is."

I look to Sam to take the lead because I'm not sure if he wants to tell Denise that we were spending time together.

"We walked into town for a snow cone," he states simply. I guess it's not a secret like I thought it would be.

"What? You got a snow cone while I got cried on! I had to give her a dose of her sleeping medicine to get her to take a nap."

"Oh, so she's out for a while?" I ask.

"Yeah, she'll probably be out for the rest of the night. I already texted Dad to let him know."

"Do you guys want to go get dinner and then watch the sunset on the beach?" I ask, bracing myself for them both to say no.

"Yeah," they say in unison surprising me.

A half hour later, after we all freshen up, we take an uber to the other side of the island, close to where Piku Ranch is. I wonder what time Ethan gets off. The three of us go back and forth about where to eat. In the end Sam and I give up the battle, letting Denise decide on some Italian place.

The restaurant is quaint and serene, with statues and a coin fountain. I'm glad I decided on my jean skirt and a nice black beaded blouse. We get a table beside the fountain, feeling the spritz of water fall on us. The server brings a basket of hot bread, quickly filling our glasses with water from the pitcher he is carrying. I see Denise eye the guy like he's an appetizer. He introduces himself as Sergio. Looking over the menu, the spinach ravioli in alfredo sauce sounds amazing. Denise does the shrimp scampi, to watch her calories, she claims, and Samson gets the lobster ravioli. It's nice sitting here, having dinner, making small talk over the attractive server Denise wants to pack up in a to-go box. When he drops off our meals, she gives his arm a squeeze.

"Would you want to take me out on Friday night?" she asks confidently.

"It just so happens to be my night off. I'm down." Sergio smiles at her.

"Cool. Here's my number. Text me." She winks.

He disappears, leaving us with a gloating Denise and amazing pasta. This is some of the best ravioli I have ever eaten. I will have to bring Ethan here, hopefully he likes Italian food. I devour mine, dipping a slice of bread in the extra sauce. *Delizioso*! Denise eats tiny bites of hers, cutting the angel hair with a knife, trying to appear proper, when I know damn well, she will be eating that cold, out of the box, in her pajamas, at midnight. Sam keeps the small talk going between the three of us until Sergio comes back.

"How will the bill be tonight?" he asks professionally.

"Three separate," I say at the exact same time that Sam is telling him that Denise will take the bill.

126

"She wanted to treat us to a nice Italian dinner tonight. Thanks, sis." He smiles at Sergio while wrapping his arm over Denise's shoulders.

"Oh, I see. Very considerate of you beautiful. Here you go." Sergio hands her the bill.

"What the fuck, Sammy!" she whispers, once Sergio has walked away.

"You wanted to eat here. It's only fair that you pay the check." He tells her, finishing his last bite.

"*Uggghhhh!*" She digs her card out of her purse, it's not like it's her own money. That is Uncle Dan's credit card she is handing over.

Once we leave the restaurant, we only have to walk a couple of blocks down the street until we get to an opening for access to the beach. The sun is sinking into the ocean, painting the sky an orangey-pink color, like rainbow sherbet. The sky behind us is blue and purple, night approaching, soon to encapsulate the island. The three of us walk in the sand, watching our toes sink beneath the grains. I find a level spot on the ground, to watch the last of the sun, with Sam and Denise taking seats on either side of me. A new trio of friends watching the sunset on Kauai is something I never thought could happen.

"Zoey?" a familiar voice calls behind me, causing me to twist my torso around at lightning speed.

"Ethan!" I yell, jumping up to run over to him. I wrap my arms around his neck, kissing him hard on the mouth. He is dressed in his bright green work uniform with splatters of mud all over him.

"Wow. Miss me?" He quirks his eyebrow at me.

"Yeah. What are you doing here?" I say, bashfully.

"I was just driving home from work when I thought I saw

you, so I pulled over. Turns out it really is you."

"Oh, you thought you saw me so you pulled over, what if it was a total stranger? I think it's you who missed me." I joke, making him smile.

"Of course, I missed my *maka nani.*"

That's the second time he's called me that. Before I can ask what it means, I feel Denise right beside me.

"Hi, I'm Denise. Nice to finally meet you," she flirts with him, causing me to roll my eyes.

"Ethan," he tells her flatly, remembering her from the ATV tour. He didn't seem to like her much then and doesn't appear to now either. It makes my heart skip a beat knowing that someone has finally chosen me over Denise.

"I'm Samson, but you can call me Sam," he chirps behind me, breaking up the unease of Denise.

They shake hands, Ethan telling him it's nice to meet him. Such a gentleman.

"We came out for dinner and to watch the sunset," I tell him. He raises his eyebrows at me, surprised. The cousins walk back to where we were sitting and I whisper to Ethan, "They have been nice to me lately. I invited them to dinner and they came. Denise even paid for me."

"Maybe they have come to realize how special you are to have in their lives." His eyes sparkle.

"Do you want to stay and watch the sunset with us?" I ask hopeful.

"Sure thing," he tells me taking my hand to walk back to the others. I sit beside Denise with Ethan to my right.

Denise speaks up. "You're welcome by the way," she directs toward Ethan.

"For what?" he asks, unsure.

"I'm the one who took the picture."

"What picture?" asks Sam.

"She was trying on lingerie for Ethan and we took a picture, I sent it to him. She looked hot." She throws all my business out there in the open. Sam looks like he is going to get sick. He shoots me a look that apologizes for his sister.

"Too much information, sis."

"You were trying the lingerie on for me specifically?" Ethan whispers in my hair as Denise and Samson bicker about exploiting personal information.

I don't think I can turn any redder. "Maybe."

"Can I go with you, the next time you try some on?"

I look up into his eyes with his naughty thought. "Of course." I grin.

We sit there until the sun sinks completely into the ocean. Ethan is the first to stand up.

"I've got to get going, Zo. Do you guys have a ride?" Ethan asks.

"Yeah, our Uber is five minutes out," Samson informs him.

"Cool," he replies. "Walk me to my car?" he asks, hinting that he wants to talk to me alone.

When we get to the parking lot, he leans against his driver-side door. "You're sure everything is good with them?" he asks looking over my shoulder.

"Yeah, I've been talking with both of them. Things are going okay. It's nice actually."

"Okay." Dropping the topic, he gives me his million-dollar grin. "Can I sneak over later?"

"Yes, please," I nod, not caring who is watching, I press my body into his, brushing my lips against the corner of his mouth. He seals a kiss, softly touching his tongue to mine.

"Eh hem! If you're going to fuck, get a hotel room!" Denise shouts, interrupting the moment. I can hear Samson smack her arm and her fuss with him. I pull away.

"I'll see you in a little bit," Ethan whispers against my lips. "The door will be open."

As Ethan is getting in the Jeep, a grey Honda civic pulls in for us. Perfect timing.

The ride home is quiet. All of us are tired. I concentrate on getting home and figuring out what to wear to bed that could look somewhat sexy for Ethan. As soon as we pull into the driveway, I hurry to my room bidding goodnight to Denise and Sam. I run my brush through my hair and brush my teeth. I am still in the bathroom when he appears at the sliding door, nearly giving me a heart attack as I walk into the bedroom to see him standing there.

"Shit!" I squeal, clutching my chest as I double over trying to calm my racing heart.

"Sorry. I didn't want to knock in case anyone was still awake and heard it."

"It's okay," I tell him walking over to the bed, I climb under the covers waiting for him to join me.

"You, ma'am, are causing me issues," he tells me sternly. I panic, not knowing what I did.

"What did I do?" I ask, thinking he is mad at me.

He pulls his shirt off, revealing my hickey on his chest. "Remember how I had to change shirts at work this morning? Yeah, well Jeremy and Liam were in the break room too."

He pulls out his phone, clicking on something before handing it to me. My hand shoots up to cover my mouth. It's a picture of his back with eight red lines across his shoulders.

"You marked me. The boys have been giving me hell all day,

130

it has me frustrated," he tells me, giving me a sexy little grin. He's not really mad at me. What a relief. For a minute I thought I had messed everything up. I crawl across the bedspread to snag my fingers in the waistband of his shorts. I lean into his bare chest, giving him puppy dog eyes as I stare up at him.

"Is there anything I can do to help ease your frustration?" I ask slowly, drawing circles across his chest with the tip of my finger. I smile up at him, leaning down to press a kiss against the purple mark on his pectoral muscle. I flick my tongue against his nipple noticing his hands finding their way to my hips. I continue my path up his neck, sucking on his collar bone but he pushes me back.

"Not my neck, you damn vampire." He laughs.

"Same goes for you! I had to borrow makeup from Denise to cover mine!" I say, poking him.

He traces his finger over the spot where he left his mark. He knew exactly where he left it. I climb off the bed going into the bathroom for a wet washcloth, rubbing it over my neck to remove the makeup. When I return to the spot I was in, he rubs his thumb over my hickey.

"There it is. Why did you cover it?" he asks, almost sounding hurt.

"I didn't want to hide it, but I knew the wrath I would face from my aunt if she saw it. I couldn't handle any more of her comments today." I look down to avoid his gaze, thinking about her calling me a slut earlier.

"What did she do?" he asks cautiously, taking my hands in his. I blink back the tears.

"She said I was a slut for spending so much time with you. Uncle Dan invited you and me to a luau with them on Sunday and she freaked out. Told me there was no room in the car for sluts and that I better not make a scene or ruin her luau."

Ethan climbs on the bed in front of me so that he is facing me on his knees.

"I really hate your aunt."

"I do too."

"You're not a slut. Denise maybe, but not you. Do you want to go to the luau on Sunday?"

"Yeah. I'm getting along with everyone else besides my aunt. Can you come with me? It's okay if you're busy or have plans or something." I look away, prepared for rejection.

"I wouldn't miss it. You are allowed in my car so I will pick you up. Do you have a dress for it yet?"

"No, I don't think anything I have would be suitable for a luau."

"How about we go shopping tomorrow? Maybe grab some dinner before the bonfire," he asks, kissing my cheek.

"Yes please," I nod, tilting my head to expose my neck to his mouth.

He brushes his mouth over the exposed flesh, making the hair stand up on the back of my neck. I run my hands over his back, scratching my nails over his sides, making him hiss in pleasure. His hands smooth over my hips, up to the clasp of my bra, freeing my breasts of the unwanted binding. His large warm hands cover each breast, grazing over the sensitive bud of my hardened nipples.

"Ethan." I break the kiss to whisper into the darkened room.

He reaches behind him, pulling his wallet from his back pocket, snatching a condom out.

"The last one," he says holding it up.

"Just until tomorrow. We'll buy more when we go shopping," I say, pulling the front of his shorts open. He kicks them off behind him. I lay on my back in the middle of the bed slipping my underwear down my legs. I crawl back up to my knees to meet him for a kiss. He grabs a fistful of my hair to pull my head back so he can attack my neck. Looks like I'll need some more of Denise's cover-up in the morning. He presses me back into the mattress, taking his time, warming me up. He uses his fingers to get me to fall apart before entering me. I gasp as the internal ache fades away, pleasure consuming me, knowing this is exactly what I need. His arms lock underneath my back, holding me as close as possible to him as his hips meet mine. He kisses me with a passion that makes my stomach flutter. He speeds up, thrusting into me, his pubic bone rubbing against my clit in the most earth-shattering feeling. I can hear his balls slapping in the wetness that's dripping out of me. Another orgasm racks my body as I am listening to that sound. My back arches off the bed, my legs squeeze around him while I'm coming undone. He thrusts deep one last time, unloading himself into the latex barrier separating us.

"You feel so good inside of me," I whisper, running my fingers through his hair as he catches his breath. I feel him twitch when I say that. He pulls out, disposing of the condom. I get up to pee then crawl under the covers with Ethan.

"For losing your virginity yesterday, you are very horny." He smiles at me.

I blush, embarrassed. "Sorry. I... I really like having sex with you."

"No need. I have to restrain myself from fucking you every time I see you," he says boldly, his words making me blush.

"Do you? I know I'm not experienced like the other girls you've been with, so I don't really know what to do or what you like."

"Just ask me. We can experiment whenever you're ready. We can talk about it."

"Yes, please," I whisper burying my head in his arm.

"Hey, you don't need to be embarrassed. You and I can talk about anything. We've technically known each other our whole lives. What do you want to know?"

"Is sex with me actually good for you or were you just saying that?"

"Look at me," he says, pulling my chin up to peer into my eyes. "I have never enjoyed sex so much in my life. You're tight and get so wet for me. It's more than just sex with you though. There's a connection that makes it so much better."

"What do you think about during it?" I ask my next question.

"You. I wonder if you're enjoying it or if you're imagining Taylor Lautner instead of me. I'm trying to learn where your spots are, the ones that really turn you on."

"I only think about you. You are a dream come true. I can tell you my spots. At least the ones I know about so far."

"Where are your spots?"

"My nipples, my neck, I like when you grab my hair, I really liked what you did with your mouth in the Jeep," I list off for him.

"Oral sex is fucking awesome. I loved tasting you."

"I really like when you cuss. Is that weird? It turns me on."

"No. Lots of people like dirty talk. I am also one of those people," he informs me.

"You like it too?" I ask, surprised.

"Oh yeah. I want to hear what you want me to do to you."

"Me too." I smile thinking it's nice we have this in common. "What do you like?"

"I like when you pull my hair, when you dig your nails into

134

my ass and when you say my name."

"Ethan," I breathe out.

"Yeah. This is going to make me sound like a *lolo*; I like that you were a virgin. It means there is so much more to explore, and it's really selfish of me but I want to be the one you explore with."

"I want you to be that one too. I have many curiosities so I hope you are down for a challenge."

"Shootz," he responds. I yawn, drowsiness setting in.

"Let's get some sleep. We have all day tomorrow," he tells me.

"Okay. Goodnight, Ethan." I press a kiss against his chest, snuggling my cheek against him, pulling the covers higher.

"Goodnight, Zoey."

Chapter 14

It is so warm in the room. I can feel Ethan's head resting on my chest. Sometime throughout the night, we got into this position, with his arm and leg draped over me. My arm is resting on his shoulders while my other arm holds his hand that is draped over my waist. I wish I could lay like this forever but my bladder is telling me to get up. I open my eyes as slowly as possible, only to scream bloody murder when I see Denise standing in the room. Of course, Ethan bolts awake in the bed, looking ready to fight someone with his bed head, only to set eyes on her.

"What are you doing in here?" I shriek, clutching the blanket to my chest. Ethan sits beside me, rubbing the sleep out of his eyes, looking pissed.

"I have a pimple and need my blemish stick back. You should really lock the door if you're going to sneak a boy home."

Ugh! I forgot to lock the door last night.

"It's in the bathroom," I groan at her. She walks in, grabs it, comes right back to the bedroom, and sits on the edge of the bed. Both of us are naked and she decides now is the time for a heart-to-heart.

"So, how was it?" she asks in a teasing tone.

"God, would you please leave?" I beg.

"You're lucky Mom and Dad aren't home. Sammy just went to call Aiden."

"The sex is fucking amazing, all right?" I let out, frustrated that she is making me answer the question. If it will shut her up and get her out of this room, I will tell her anything at this point.

"That's all I needed to hear. Catch you guys later," she says, leaving. I groan, throwing myself back down into the pillows. Ethan does the same.

"Fucking amazing, huh?" he questions with a shit-eating grin.

"Jesus." I laugh, climbing out of bed. Once my teeth are brushed and hair pulled up into a high ponytail, I walk back into the bedroom naked, slipping into a black bra and panty set. I put on my black mini skirt, my new teal Kauai shirt, and my sky-blue sequined flip flops.

Ethan comes up behind me, wrapping his arms around me, his presence calming my irritation.

"I would have taken care of your frustration with my mouth if you hadn't run off," he says sensually in my ear while rubbing his palm between my thighs. My head falls back on his shoulder wishing more than anything a magical condom would appear from thin air.

"Come on." My stomach growling breaks the silence. Since Denise knows he is here, there is no point in sneaking out of the garden door, so I take him out through the kitchen. I don't feel like hanging around for any more of Denise's questions, so I offer to buy us breakfast in town. After some pancakes and orange juice, we go to the boutique I shopped at the other day with Denise. Finding ourselves alone in the lingerie, I turn on the charm.

"Pick me something out. I'll try on anything you want to see," I whisper in his ear, biting his earlobe.

I watch as Ethan wanders through rack after rack of laces and corsets. He seems just as confused as me by the ones that look like it would take multiple people to strap it on. He chooses a purple corset with glitter in the material, a black lace bodysuit, and my favorite, a pink and orange baby doll that is see-through, with orange feathers skirted around the bottom. It looks like a Hawaiian sunset. I grab his hand, pulling him to the dressing rooms. Thank God it's the kind of dressing room where the door extends from the ceiling to the floor with no opening to see in. I sit Ethan down in a chair outside of my changing room, making him wait in anticipation. I start with the black body suit, not thinking highly of it. It compliments my ass, but it's way too baggy in the chest. I don't bother showing it to Ethan. The glittery purple one is hot. It squeezes my breasts together but also takes the air from my lungs. I crack open the door to see his head jerk up from staring at his phone. I can see his eyebrows shoot into his hairline, shifting in his seat.

"What do you think?" I ask seductively.

"I think you should let me in that dressing room with you," he says, eyes not leaving my chest.

"But I still have one more to try on." I notice as he rubs his hand over his crotch, crossing his legs to hide his discomfort.

I twirl around, making sure he gets a view of my ass, as I close the door behind me. Time to see if this sunset baby doll suits me or not. As soon as it's on, I know that I'm buying it. It flatters my newly tanned skin, making me feel sexy and confident. I stare at myself in the mirror admiring the way the orange feathers brush against my bare pussy, I didn't bother to put on the thong that goes with it. I hope Ethan loves it as much as I do. Taking a deep breath, I grab the handle, turning it until the door pops open.

Ethan's eyes go wide, jaw hitting the floor. His gaze wanders up and down, over my body, then he turns his head, and looking to the left and right of him. Before I know what he is doing, he surges into the dressing room with me, pressing me into the mirror, kicking the door closed with his foot.

"We are buying this one. I want you to wear it while you ride me," he whispers, making me pussy clench with the dirty thought of being on top of him. I can't make eye contact as I summon the courage to tell him exactly what I want.

"I want you to make me come with your mouth."

With a huge grin, he drops to his knees in front of me, pulling my knee over his shoulder. I can't believe he's actually doing this right now. He kisses my pussy, edging closer to spread me open. I watch as he dives in with his tongue, targeting my clit with full force. Feeling his finger rub against me before sinking into my center, I tug his hair between my fingers, letting him devour me. It doesn't take long before I'm trembling against the dressing room wall, orgasming around his finger. His tongue laps over my clit, drawing out my orgasm. I feel like collapsing as Ethan lowers my leg off his shoulder, standing up. He moves his finger to his mouth, the one that was inside of me, sucking my arousal off.

"That was amazing," I whisper in a haze of stars.

"Is everything all right in there?" a store clerk calls through the door.

"Yeah. Everything is fine. I'll be up to the register in a minute," I reply in a shaky voice.

"All right, I will meet you up there," she says, hearing her heels click against the tile as she walks away.

Ethan is laughing as I remove myself from the wall.

"Out. Let me get dressed." I laugh, pushing him toward the door.

"Like I haven't seen you naked," he smirks, exiting the changing room.

Walking up to the checkout desk, Ethan walks behind me, grabbing at my butt. We get to the counter and the woman smiles at us.

"*Aloha*, I didn't see you back there, young man," she speaks. I think she just busted us, but Ethan covers quickly.

"I was browsing through the racks, giving her some privacy," he says smoothly.

"Oh, okay. I must have missed you."

I set the two lingerie outfits on the counter, watching as she removes the security tag, folding them carefully into one of their fancy bags.

"$35.89," she says, reading me the total. I swipe my card, rushing to get out of this awkward moment. I snatch my bag off the counter bidding her a good afternoon. I grab Ethan's hand, racing toward the exit. When we get out onto the sidewalk, I grab his arm again, dying of laughter. He grabs hold of me, laughing too.

"We almost got caught… doing that… in the dressing room," I squeal. My adrenaline is rushing. Being with Ethan is thrilling, full of excitement and sexual energy. I plant a kiss against his mouth before turning back to the sidewalk.

"Where to next?" he asks.

"Convenience store," I say quickly, causing him to laugh.

When we walk in, the same creepy guy from Tuesday is there. I give him a big smile, gloating at the need for more condoms. We stroll to the condom aisle together, not hiding anything this time. I didn't realize how many different condom options there were. Some say *ribbed*, some say *her pleasure*, while others are *glow in the dark*. Ethan reaches for another three-pack of Magnums. I shake my head, putting them back on the shelf. I grab the value box of twenty, earning a naughty glance from Ethan.

"What? You started it." I smile.

He smiles mischievously. "This is gonna be fun."

The guy at the counter recognizes us when we approach.

"Back for more, huh?" He laughs obnoxiously. Something about this guy really creeps me out.

"Well, if you had one the size of his, you'd need the value box too." I snark at him.

The smile instantly drops off his face. Ethan coughs behind me, hiding his laugh. The creep rings us out and I hand him a ten, not waiting around for the 13 cents change.

"You're hot when you're pissed," he tells me.

"That guy is a creep. I feel like he imagines me naked and it's weird. What time is the bonfire tonight?" I ask.

"We usually meet up around eight p.m."

"Okay, so we have a while. What do you want to do?" It's only one fifteen p.m. right now.

"Can we just visit a bunch of beaches?" I ask, looking for an easy day.

"That sounds perfect."

We beach hop, up until dinner where we stop at this roadside burger joint. They have a secret recipe dip for their fries. It was absolutely *ono*! I might have to buy a bottle of that sauce before I return to Michigan. I'm excited to meet all of Ethan's friends. We park away from all the cars in the parking lot, enjoying the longer walk with the sunset.

We are the last ones to arrive at the bonfire, the sun having already disappeared. There is a group of people sitting in a circle around a huge fire, built seven feet into the air. I recognize Jeremy and Liam. Zach is there, holding a guy's hand, presumably his husband that he had mentioned at the tattoo shop, and Keloni, from the helicopter. There are also a couple of girls, sharing a blanket on the sand. When we walk up, Jeremy and Liam start whistling.

"There she is!" Jeremy yells excitedly. *Oh god. What did I get myself into?*

"You got to take it easier on our boy. He's fragile," Liam yells out, laughing. Ethan flips him off. He walks over to a blue cooler full of beer, grabbing one for himself, then looking at me questioning. What the hell? I give him a nod, reaching my hand out. My first ever drink is a Big Wave Golden Ale, a local beer that's brewed here on the island. Something about this just feels right.

"What are you guys talking about?" Zach asks, missing the jokes.

Jeremy explains, "Ethan came to work covered in scratch marks and a hickey. His girl plays rough. Sent him a dirty pic too, he fell into a ditch looking at it." Boy, he doesn't keep anything to himself, he's just like Denise. Ethan looks ready to drown him. I'm not bothered by any of their jabs. *What's the big deal if I have a little fun with Ethan? We're only young once, right?*

Everyone is now eyeballing me. "What? He's amazing in bed," I tell them, nudging his shoulder. He drops his head but I see a smile.

"He is. His tongue can work some magic, if you know what I mean." Enter girl one. A feisty redhead, with freckles scattered like stars across her face. She is one of the girls sitting on the blanket. Her breasts are overflowing from a red bikini top, looking desperate for a guy's attention. She is skinny and I can tell she is tall even from seeing her sitting down. Must be one of the exes. I can handle this.

"Kaitlyn." Ethan snaps beside me.

"What? Are we supposed to hide our history from your new playmate?"

"She's not a playmate. She's actually girlfriend material," Ethan defends me. I can see the anger on his face.

"Oh! Girlfriend! Her pussy must be magic."

Before Ethan can say anything else, I let myself speak up, unrestrained.

"Well, there's a reason he's fucking me now, instead of you," I tell her hotly. The guys' eyes shoot up, impressed by my comeback. Ethan wraps his arm around my shoulders.

"Enough, ladies. Let's play a game. Truth or dare!" Jeremy yells. I can tell he's already had a few drinks.

Liam is the first to chime in, appearing to have had as much to drink as Jeremy. "Truth."

"If you could fuck one celebrity, who would it be?" Jeremy asks.

"Jennifer Lawrence," Liam answers as if he's thought about this before.

"Dude! You have a girlfriend, one who looks nothing like Jennifer Lawrence," Keloni tells him.

"Yeah, and we have a deal. Should I ever have the chance to sleep with J Law, I get a pass," Liam states.

"And what does Erica get in return?" Keloni asks.

"She's allowed to fuck Hero Fiennes Tiffin, if the opportunity presents itself."

"Who's that?"

"The dude from that *After* series she's obsessed with." Liam gruffs.

"I feel like she and I would be good friends," I tell Liam, also loving that series. Ethan glances at me and I shrug. What can

I say? I'm a hopeless romantic.

"Truth or dare?" Liam asks the group.

"Dare," says the Asian chick next to Kaitlyn, with smooth black hair, and flawless winged eyeliner.

"All right, Mya, I dare you to shotgun a beer," Liam tells her, pulling an unopened can from the cooler, handing it over to her.

She uses her car key to cut a hole in the bottom of the can, cracking open the top. She downs it fast, crushing the empty can in her fist, tossing it at him. Impressive.

"Truth or dare?" she asks, letting out a loud belch.

"Dare," says the guy holding Zach's hand. Zach introduced him as Mikala when we arrived.

"Mika, no baby," Zach groans.

"I dare you to dance like Rihanna in her Umbrella music video." Mya laughs.

"Done!" Mikala says, standing up, searching for something on the ground, only to come back with a long stick he is holding like an umbrella. Zach looks mortified. I catch his glance.

"Every week, he chooses dare. And every week someone dares him to dance." He explains.

"You know you love it," Mikala shouts, interrupting his chorus.

When he finishes his dance, he sits down, out of breath, grabbing a fresh drink. "Truth or dare?"

"Dare," Ethan speaks up for his turn. Oh, this should be good.

"I dare you to strip naked and swim out to the buoy." *Oh. Okay.* They turned it up a notch for Ethan, I see. This makes me not want a turn.

"Come on, man," Ethan groans.

144

"It's nothing we haven't seen before," says Kaitlyn mockingly.

He looks at me for a sign of what to do. "Let's see it," I grin, making the group cheer.

"Ugh." He stands, walking over to the edge of the water. He starts with pulling his shirt over his head, then slides his shorts off. With one look back at me, he drops his boxers. The boys whoop and holler at him. I smile, giving him a *shaka* in approval. Kaitlyn decides to attack while Ethan is gone.

"Ethan and I? We used to fuck. A lot. Until his daddy issues became too much for me to handle, so I had to cut him loose. If I were you, I'd stop wasting my time now."

I whip my head around to glare at her. *Did she seriously just say that?* I feel the blood rushing to my head. *How dare she speak of Ethan or his father that way!* His family is my family by several newly found connections so I feel the need to defend them. But for Ethan's sake, I force myself to take a deep breath before I cause a scene.

"The only way I'm wasting my time is by speaking to you," I respond, keeping my cool. I won't let her get to me. The rest of the group is flicking their eyes between me and her, not knowing what to say or do. You could cut the tension with a knife. As Ethan swims up the shore, we get a full-frontal view of him. My eyes light up but so do hers. Hers with menace behind them.

"I do miss that cock of his. He used to pull out and come on my tits. It was so hot," she tells me.

I roll my eyes, refusing to acknowledge her antics, when internally I want to destroy her. She's the selfish one who left Ethan after he brought her home. She's the one who hurt him.

Ethan comes strolling up, giving the boys a big 'fuck you' as he sits down beside me, laughing.

"Truth or dare?" he asks, taking a swig of his beer.

"Dare," Kaitlyn responds flirtingly. He rolls his eyes.

"I dare you to suck your big toe," Zach chirps up, saving Ethan from her games.

"Gross. No."

"You know the rules. Refuse a dare, take a shot," he tells her, offering her a bottle of rum.

She takes it, gulping more than a shot, straight from the bottle. "Truth or dare?" she asks.

This is my moment. "Dare." I take my turn before anyone else speaks up. She gives me a twisted smile, letting me know that I've fallen into her trap.

"I dare you to blow Ethan behind that tree over there," she says, pointing to a wide palm tree in a small grove of trees and bushes.

"Fuck no," Ethan tells her.

"Why? Is she bad at it? I'd be happy to suck you off myself," she says.

"Come on, Kaitlyn," Liam begs.

"Take a shot then," she says, passing the bottle in my direction.

Instead of grabbing the bottle, I stand up, looking around at everyone, then down to Ethan, offering him my hand. "I thought the dare was supposed to be something we didn't want to do. Come on, babe," I say, staring into his face.

He looks ready to run back into the ocean. I've completely caught him off guard. Jeremy gives a big howl, encouraging Ethan to go. He stands up, eyeing me cautiously.

"We'll be back." I smile at the group, noticing Kaitlyn looking annoyed that her plan failed, clearly not expecting me to go through with it. All we hear are hoots and whistles as we disappear into a thick of trees, along with Kaitlyn's voice telling everyone to fuck off.

"Zoey, we don't have to do this. Let's leave. It's just a stupid game, and Kaitlyn's being a bitch," he tells me when we're alone.

I back him up against the tree bringing my lips close to his.

"I want to," I whisper looking into his eyes. I can see his pupils dilate in surprise.

"But here? Now?" he questions, trying to talk me out of it.

Instead of replying, I bring my lips to his. My fingers find their way into his hair, tugging slightly until he starts to respond. I can tell he is still unsure by the slow pace at which he kisses me back. I rub my hands over his chest, pulling back to move my lips to his ear.

"Can I please suck your cock?" I say, asking for permission. Hook, line, sinker.

"Zoey," he whines. "You've never done this before."

"I'm ready to learn. Just guide me. Let me know what you like," I tell him, feigning confidence that I might do this right.

He pulls my chin up, meeting my gaze. "Fine, but if you want to stop at any time, just stop, okay?" he says defeated.

I nod my head, slipping my hand beneath the waistband of his shorts. I resume kissing him, waiting until I feel him get hard in my hand, before dropping to my knees. He looks down at me, making me feel so erotic and sexy. *God, I hope I'm good at this.* I want to pleasure him the way he does me. I unzip his shorts, swiftly pulling his boxers down with them, leaving his erection exposed to the breeze.

"Jesus," he gasps, I haven't even touched him yet. I grab the base of his shaft with my hand, giving him a couple of pumps before slowly closing my lips around the tip. It's salty but in a way that makes you crave more. I slide my mouth over the length

147

of him, hearing him curse when he hits the back of my throat. My eyes water, but it fades quickly. I slide my tongue against the underside of him, swirling around the tip, just like my Cosmo magazines taught me. Using my other hand, I squeeze his balls gently, earning a moan from Ethan. I rub my tongue through the opening on the tip, feeling him twitch with the sensation, getting a bigger drop of cum that time. It has an almost citrus flavor to it, salty but fruity. He's absolutely delicious. His fingers are in my hair, tangling in the strands, guiding my head down to swallow him.

"God, I'm about to lose it. You can spit or swallow, I don't care," he informs me, knowing that I have no clue what to do with it. An idea pops into my head and I know exactly what I'm going to do. I suck a little harder on the tip, sliding my hand over his slick shaft a bit faster. His body tenses, tightening his grip on my hair to where it's almost painful.

"I'm coming," he groans, spurting his release into my mouth. The tang is sweet. I swallow a little but collect the rest in my mouth. I wait for him to finish, before standing up with a mouth full of his sperm. He notices my face in his orgasmic bliss and his face contorts in confusion.

"Do you still have… in your mouth… what are you doing? Where are you going?" I give him a nod, marching back in the direction of the bonfire. There are cheers when I appear, with a satisfied smirk on my face, concealing what I have in my mouth.

"Woah! Dude, no way! That wasn't even ten minutes!" Jeremy shouts.

"They didn't do anything," yells Mikala.

"He finishes fast," Liam jokes.

"There's no way they did anything. He never came that fast with me," Kaitlyn states.

148

Ethan comes running up behind me, tugging his zipper up in the process, earning more applause. I make my way over to Kaitlyn, standing directly over her, I spit his cum onto her cleavage. The cheers die, silence filling the beach as if someone had just died.

"What the fuck?" Kaitlyn squeals, jumping to her feet. She smears her finger through it, trying to figure out the substance. *"Ewww!* What is that?" she shrieks, the slimy substance dripping down her chest.

"You said you missed his cum on your tits," I reply. The entire group loses their shit. Ethan looks confused behind me, having missed the earlier conversation. I'll have to fill him in later. But right now? This is my revenge for her comments earlier.

"You bitch! You're dead!" she screams, lunging for me.

I duck, evading her blow, then with a single swing, my fist connects with her cheekbone, knocking her into the sand.

"Five years of MMA. Try again, bitch," I yell. Finally, after all of those training classes, my skills have paid off. My dad insisted I learn how to protect myself. Turns out, I am pretty good with mixed martial arts. Everyone is going crazy. I squat down to look her in the eyes as I say what comes next.

"If you ever say anything about Ethan or his family again, you'll be covered in blood next time instead of cum," I tell her through my teeth, getting the point across that I mean it.

Ethan is behind me suddenly, pulling my arms to get me up.

"Come on. Let's go," he tells me. I'm ready for more. Let that bitch come at me.

He guides me in the direction of the Jeep as my heartbeats out of my chest. I am so high on this victory; I want to relish in it. It's upsetting that Ethan is pulling me away until my back meets the side of the Jeep and he is flush against me, kissing me hard. It's hot. He ravishes my mouth, one hand gripping my ass while the other tangles in my hair holding my face to his. In a rush, he breaks away.

"What the fuck was that?" Escapes from his mouth.

"When you were in the water, she said some stuff about you. I couldn't let her get away with it. I'm sorry," I reply.

"What did she say?" he asks, taking a step back, preparing to hear the worst.

"She made comments about you having daddy issues and that's why she had to let you go. Said she missed your cum on her tits when you'd pull out of her," I tell him softly.

"So that's why you spit it on her?" he asks.

"Kinda." I reply hesitantly. Without warning his lips are consuming mine.

"Thank you. For defending me," he tells me.

"You're welcome," I whisper, kissing him again.

"We need to find someplace. I need you. If that's all right?" his eyes appear glazed over in a hormone-fueled frenzy.

I turn, gesturing to his Jeep. The top is on right now so we could do it inside without anyone seeing.

"I've never had anyone in my Jeep," he states breathlessly, looking at the orange vehicle behind me.

"Okay. If you don't want to, we can go back to my place—" I can't finish my sentence before he interrupts.

"No, I want you to be the first. Get in."

I climb in, sliding across the seat to give him room. As soon as he sits down, I straddle him, moving my hands down to unbuckle his pants, opening them enough to get him out. I kiss his neck as I stroke him in my hand. His nails dig into my thighs, but it pushes me further. Just as I'm moving my panties to the side to sink down on him, I remember he's not wearing a condom. Shit. Quickly, I crawl over the middle console, grab the box from the front floor-boards, rip it open and toss him one. As soon as he slips it over himself, I retake my position on top of him, lowering myself onto his hardness.

It's different in this position. I use my thighs to propel myself up and down on the car's seat. It's empowering riding him like this, like I have what he needs and only I can give it to him. He seems like he's enjoying it also, face level with my breasts, watching them bounce as I ride him. His fingers keep clenching into my thighs, pulling me against him. I feel like a porn star on him, squeezing my own tits and pulling my hair. The sexual nymph inside has been released. The windows are steaming up, causing sweat to run down the side of my face. I know I'm close but I'm not sure about him. To get him to catch up to me, I bite his ear and whisper, "Fuck me, I want you to cum," he growls and I swear it's the hottest thing ever. He is covered in sweat from both of us. He starts thrusting up into me, hitting my G-spot. I scream his name, not caring who hears, as he thrusts harder, filling the condom. He slows down, relaxing back in the seat as I snuggle under his chin, feeling him soften inside of me. I climb off him, pull the condom off and tie it, to avoid spilling his seed in the Jeep. He pulls me back against him, kissing me hard on the mouth.

"Car sex is hot," he says with a grin.

"I'm glad I could be your first," I reply happily.

"What you did on the beach… that shit turned me on… you spit my cum on my ex-girlfriend defending me and my family… I've never… Fuck, if I wasn't so hot, we'd go for round two," he says, making my pussy twitch. Zipping up his pants, and jumping into the driver seat, he turns on the Jeep, cranking up the AC. We roll the windows down, letting the fog clear. My phone starts buzzing on the floorboards in the back seat. I maneuver over the armrest to grab it, getting a smack against my ass that's sticking up in the air. I smile and swat his hand, looking down at the screen, I see it's Denise. That's weird. Isn't she supposed to be on her date with Sergio?

"Hello?" I ask warily.

"Zoey?" she sounds vulnerable, as if she's crying.

"What's wrong?" I ask, expecting someone to have gotten hurt. Ethan looks at me, trying to listen in.

"Sergio was a total douche. He tried to get in my pants and when I said no, he pushed me out of his car and drove off. I don't know where I am at. Do you think you could come and get me?"

I look at him worried. I put her on speaker so Ethan can hear her better.

"What's around you?" he asks, putting the Jeep into reverse, backing out of the parking spot.

"Um, there is a clothing store down the street called Pilo Pattie. I think I see a Walmart in the distance or something with a big blue sign. Other than that, not much."

"I know where you're at. Stay there, under a street lamp. We are going to stay on the phone with you, don't hang up." Ethan speeds down the road, hitting the mute button on my phone so that Denise can't hear him.

"She's in a bad area. We only have one Walmart and where she's at, has a lot of homeless people and gang violence from the drug scene."

"Oh shit," I say, panic setting in.

"Hey. We are going to get to her," he says sternly, grabbing my hand.

I talk to Denise as we drive, trying to keep her occupied. I

152

find out that Sergio took her to the restaurant he worked at for dinner, making her pay the bill since he supposedly forgot his wallet. He took her to an empty parking lot to hook up but when she said no, he shoved her out of the car, leaving her stranded.

"Zoey. There is a group of guys walking this way," she says, scared.

"How many are there?" I panic, sitting forward as if it will speed up the drive. Ethan puts his foot to the floor, doing thirty over the limit. Please let his uncle be the one on duty if we get pulled over.

"There's six of them. I think they just spotted me." I can hear catcalls and whistles in the background. I glance at Ethan to see his mouth in a firm line and his knuckles turning white on the wheel.

"We're almost there," he tells her.

"Please hurry," she cries.

We take a sharp left off a side road, landing us on a main drag, seeing a figure standing under a street lamp with a group approaching her. Ethan races up, tires squealing to a halt under the lamppost.

"Get in," he yells, hitting the unlock button for the doors.

She throws herself in, and as soon as the door is closed, Ethan hits the lock button, just as the group of guys walk up. Ethan hits the gas, one of the guys diving out of the way before getting run over. We drive, slowing down to the regular speed limit when we get into a safer part of town. Denise sits in the back with tears rolling down the sides of her face. Ethan looks in the rearview at her, noticing her shirt is ripped. When we get to a red light on the better side of town, he breaks the silence.

"What did he do to you?" he asks carefully.

I see her break loose, letting the tears flow freely as she sobs into her hands. The most confident girl I know, the one I've never seen shed a tear, is currently drowning in them. I unbuckle, climb into the backseat with her, and wrap my arm around her shoulders. Ethan pulls over into a little parking lot of a twenty-four-hour diner. When she is out of tears, she dries her face, climbs out of the Jeep and walks into the diner. I'm confused, but I follow behind her. She sits in a booth, staring out the window into the darkness. I take the seat beside her and Ethan sits across from us. When the waitress comes, he orders three hot chocolates.

"He was rude all night, stuck me with a $250 bill at the restaurant because he apparently needed three appetizers and two desserts. When we left, I told him I wanted to go home but he drove us to an empty parking lot. He started kissing me and grabbing my breasts, squeezing so hard. I kept telling him to stop, to take me home. I was trying to open my door when he grabbed me by my shirt. He slapped me across the face, saying that if I wasn't going to put out then he was gone. He opened the door and shoved me out. I landed on my hip pretty hard, then he drove off. That's when I called you." She whimpered, with her head against the cold window glass.

"He stranded you in a bad area. It's not a good scene over there," he finally tells her.

She releases a sob, moving onto my shoulder. I stroke her hair, whispering to her that she was safe now. After a while, she sits up, wiping her ruined makeup onto a napkin, then grabs a menu.

"I am starving. Watching Sergio gorge himself killed my appetite earlier. Is it all right if I get some pancakes?" she asks like a little kid.

"Order whatever you want. Pancakes sound good. I think I'll

154

get some too." I smile, grabbing a menu for myself. I look at Ethan with a smile, giving him a look that says he better order something too. He smiles, stealing my menu.

When the waitress checks on us, Denise orders the peanut butter and banana pancakes, I get the coconut chocolate chip and Ethan orders the blueberry macadamia nut. Our food comes out fast, seeing as we are the only ones in the restaurant at this hour. When we get our plates, my mouth waters with the smell of coconut. They are fluffy, covered in whipped cream and coconut shavings, chocolate chips are cooked into the pancake itself, making them gooey and melty. We pause the conversation while we eat. These are the best pancakes ever! When we're all done, I take the bill, giving the waitress my card. Ethan drives us back to the house in silence, no one in the mood to keep up a conversation. Denise is the first to exit the car, leaving us to give me and Ethan a minute alone.

Before going into the house, Denise stops at my window to speak to Ethan.

"Thanks for coming to my rescue tonight. I know I'm not your favorite person but hopefully we can be friends," she shrugs, unsure.

"Stay away from guys like Sergio. He's a *pau 'ole*." Ethan smiles at her.

She looks confused at the Hawaiian term but walks into the house. When we're alone, Ethan brings my hand to his lips, kissing the back of it.

"Tonight was eventful," he says, lost in thought at everything that has happened.

"That's one word for it." I exhale.

"I'm sorry I can't stay tonight," he says sadly.

"It's all right. You've got to work early tomorrow. If you

155

stayed here, you wouldn't sleep."

Confused, he asks why.

"Because you'd be ridden, humped, and sucked until the sun comes up," I reply seductively.

He laughs. "Yeah, there wouldn't be much time to sleep with all of that." He lets out a chuckle.

I lean over, pressing a soft kiss against his mouth.

"I'll see you later. Goodnight." I whisper, getting out of the car.

"Goodnight."

I watch him back out of the driveway, disappearing into the darkness. I quietly slip inside my room, collapsing on my bed. I am so tired, barely managing to stand up long enough to brush my teeth and change into my pajamas, but as soon as my head hits the pillow, I am out.

Chapter 15

When I wake up Saturday morning, I am more energetic than I have been in three years. I love every minute I spend with Ethan, dreading the day I have to leave. I don't know what is going to happen yet, but I don't want to start my day off sad, so I put my thoughts aside. I put on a new pink romper with spaghetti straps and shorts up to my butt cheeks, feeling great. I head out to breakfast, to meet the rest of my family in the kitchen. Sam is sitting at the table texting who I assume is his boyfriend, due to the smile he is failing to hide. Denise and Aunt Susan are sitting at the island, each with half a grapefruit, and Uncle Dan is standing at the coffee pot with his back turned.

"Morning," I chime happily, getting the milk out of the fridge for my cereal.

Everyone mumbles a simple greeting back, except for my aunt, who has to go for my throat.

"Why are you so happy?" she gripes, scrunching her face.

"I just am," I reply, no specific reason for my happiness. It's a beautiful day. I feel good, and I am going out shopping.

"It's that boy. Probably already had you in his bed, you little tramp. You should be more like Denise. She's a good girl." I exchange a look with Denise, both of us knowing her body count.

"So, what is everyone up to today?" Uncle Dan asks, changing the subject.

No one answers, so I say, "I am going to go shopping. I need to get a dress for the luau."

Denise perks up at the mention of shopping. "Oh great. I need something too. Can I go with you?" she asks politely. Actually asking this time, instead of inviting herself. My aunt glares at her.

"Sure," I tell her happily.

"How about me?" Sam asks from across the room.

"I guess. You want to come dress shopping with us girls?" I laugh.

"I don't have anything to wear either. I'm sure one of the stores you go to will have a shirt for me," he mentions.

"Okay then," I tell him, liking that they are making an effort to build this relationship.

"I can drive you guys," my uncle states, not lifting his eyes from the newspaper.

"Am I just supposed to stay here while you all go shopping? I am going too," Aunt Susan huffs.

Ugh. My shopping trip alone has just become a family affair. I don't want to hear how fat I look in the dresses that I try on but maybe she'll be busy trying on her own dresses.

"Everyone in the car," my uncle tells us.

Samson offers to take the middle seat so I can have the window this time. It's a silent ride to the Pilo Pattie on this side of the island. I notice Samson is flipping through Snapchats from Aiden, causing him to break out into a big smile. *How can his mother not see the fact that he's in love?*

When we arrive, my aunt lets me know that I am not wearing the same matching outfit as the family, so I better find something else. I quickly disappear into the clothing racks by myself. There are Hawaiian dresses in every color, all with floral patterns, some displaying the yellow hibiscus, which I learn, is the state flower of Hawaii. I prefer the shorter dresses that go above my knee, to make me look taller than 5'4. I pick out one that is light purple with dark purple flowers. I also grab a green dress with yellow flowers. I pick two others that I don't think will look good on me, but I want to try on anyway because I like the colors.

In the dressing room, staring at myself in the mirror, I realize none of these dresses suit me. One wouldn't even pull up over my hips. One was too loose, one was too bland, and the other was just bad. I sigh, sliding my back down the dressing room wall in defeat. A few minutes go by when I hear a knock on my door.

"Zoey. It's Denise. Have you found a dress yet?" she asks.

"No," I moan back.

"I have one for you to try on," she says, surprising me. I stand up, cracking the door open since I'm still in my underwear. Though I guess it wouldn't really matter with Denise, seeing how she barged into my last dressing room when I was practically naked.

"Here. Try this." She passes me a dress through the crack. "I want to see it once it's on."

It's a white strapless dress with pink hibiscuses on it. It's short and flairs out at the waist. This dress is beautiful. The price tag is a bit expensive for me but I slip it on anyway, knowing Denise is waiting to see it. It flatters my body, making my chest look a cup size larger. I open the door to show Denise.

"Damn girl. It looks way better on you than it did on me. I knew it. You have to get it." She smiles, satisfied with her accomplishment

"I can't afford to spend $200 on a dress," I tell her, sadly, wanting this dress, but knowing I have to put it back.

My uncle walks down the row of dressing rooms at that exact moment, laying his eyes on me, overhearing our conversation.

"I'm buying. Get whatever you want. You look beautiful."

"Thank you," I gasp.

"You need shoes!" Denise squeals, running off. Uncle Dan has already vanished into his own dressing room to try on the shirts he was holding.

"Zoey! These! Here!" Denise comes running back with white heels covered in glitter.

"Me and heels don't really get along," I tell her as she forces them into my hands.

"Then introduce yourself. I bet Ethan will love them." She winks. With the mention of his name, I figure it wouldn't hurt to try them on. I am unstable in them, but with a little practice, I should be good. They do go well with this dress. Denise and I are the last to join the others at the cash register. When I go to set the dress on the counter, my aunt holds up her hand.

"What do you think you are doing?" she asks hotly.

"Dad said he would buy it for her," Denise informs her.

"I don't think so," Susan responds, handing me the dress back.

I don't understand why she hates me so much. I turn to put the dress back, bumping into Uncle Dan.

"Sorry," I mumble with my head down.

"What are you doing with that dress?" he asks.

"I can't afford it, so I'm putting it back," I tell him.

"I said I was buying it for you. What happened?" he asks, anger rising as he looks toward my aunt.

"I am not buying her a dress," she tells him.

"You're not, because I am," he states simply.

"No, you are not. It's our money, and I said no."

"No. It is my money, and I said yes. Zoey give her the dress, please," he tells me, pointing to the cashier

160

I hand it over to the clerk who scans it, placing it in a bag alongside my heels.

Nothing else is said as my uncle pays for my dress and shoes. No one says anything on the ride home either. When we get home, I take my dress and shoes, escaping into my bedroom. It really hurts to be hated for no real reason. I know I shouldn't interrupt him at work but I text Ethan to check in. He always makes me feel better.

How is work? I ask.

I lay down in bed, waiting for a response, scrolling through news articles on my phone. Fifteen minutes later I get a response.

I could use a trip to our wailele. :), he texts back. I smile.

Me too.

Everything okay?

Aunt Susan has been at me today. Just kinda down, I tell him.

She is jealous of you. You are a bright shiny star in the night sky, while she is a big, black hole. His words make me smile.

I miss you.

I miss you more. I knew he could cheer me up.

Our texts end there as I fall asleep. Maybe a nap will help me to feel better. When I wake, it's fifteen minutes after six, I've been asleep for almost four hours. I grab my phone off the pillow behind me, noticing five text messages from Ethan.

What are you up to tonight?

Is everything okay?

I just got off work. You there?

I am getting worried, Zoey.

I am on my way.

That last text was sent about twenty minutes ago. I hurry to

161

text him back, as I see him approach my garden entrance door. I hop up to unlock it, signaling that he needs to be quiet when he comes in.

"The car is gone. Is anyone home?" he asks.

They must have gone to dinner without me. I sneak out of my bedroom door to see if anyone is here.

"Hello? Is there anyone here?" I yell into the empty living room.

No answer. *Sweet.* I can have a few minutes alone with Ethan, outside of his Jeep. I walk back into my bedroom, Ethan sitting on the edge of my bed.

"I'm sorry I didn't respond. I fell asleep after our last text."

"That's fine. I overreacted and was worried," he states, embarrassed. I take a seat beside him.

"How was work?" I ask.

"It was a really good day. A customer tipped us a hundred dollars and it was just Liam and I, so we got to split it between the two of us."

"That's awesome. You guys are really good at what you do. You're super-hot too, that's got to help get tips from the ladies."

"It does." He laughs.

There is a moment of silence before I speak.

"My family went out to dinner without me," I say, hanging my head.

"I'll take you out to dinner. I haven't eaten yet either. I wanted to come check on you first."

My eyes light up hearing that I took priority over everything else.

"You came here first?" I ask.

"Of course. You are much more important," he says staring into my eyes.

I lean over, pressing my mouth into his. I kiss him with a fire, a kiss that is deep, soul binding, and a kiss that says 'thank you' for putting me first. I climb to my knees, swinging one leg over his hip, dragging my fingernails through his scalp.

"Zoey… don't start something you can't finish," he warns with a smile.

"Oh, I can make you finish. In your pants, in my mouth, inside of me," I whisper.

Groaning, he brings me back down to earth, "What if your family comes home?"

Ugh! I hate that he's right. Aunt Susan would throw me out if she caught me doing this. My head drops to his shoulder.

"You're right." I sigh.

"Hey." His hands rub over my thighs, drawing my attention. I pull my head back to look him in the eyes, "Let's get some food in you then I'll take you to our waterfall. Does that sound okay? What do you feel like eating?" he asks.

"Let's go someplace nice. I want to show off how hot you are in this romper and let the island know that you're mine," he suggests.

Ethan makes me laugh. And smile. And dream. And imagine a life I never thought I could have.

We end up dining at this Japanese grill, where they prepare the food in front of you. I get the steak, watching as they slice and cook it to medium well, with other vegetables in a delicious, teriyaki sauce. Ethan got the same and ordered a plate of sushi as an appetizer, something called the love boat. It's a small platter, with two different types of sushi. I've never had any kind of sushi though. I give it a funny look when the chef sets the plate in front of us.

"What? Don't tell me you've never had sushi before," he

states, completely shocked, using his chopsticks to pick up a piece.

"Sushi isn't really a big thing in Michigan."

"Here. Try a bite," he says, dipping it in soy sauce, and then holding it to my lips. I'll trust Ethan with anything so I take the sushi between my teeth.

It's chewy, kind of sticky on my teeth, and sour from the soy sauce. But it has cream cheese in the middle, I think I taste salmon too. It's not too bad. In fact, the more I chew, mixing the flavors, the more I dig it.

"That's pretty good!" I state, excited that I tried something new AND liked it.

"Good. Have some more. This one is salmon and that one has crab. Be careful, that green stuff is wasabi and it's really spicy," he explains the sushi to me.

I try the crab one next, dipping it in the wasabi. It's spicy, but I have had worse. There was one year, Dad challenged me to a spicy chili competition in our kitchen to see who could eat the most. Mom wasn't happy when Dad was throwing up on the bathroom floor. Ethan is staring at me funny so I ask him what's up.

"You're not crying or turning red or anything. How is that possible?"

"I like spicy foods," I tell him, saving the chili story for another time.

We snack on the sushi until our steaks are finished, the chef chopping them up and scooping them onto our plates with his knife. They are cooked perfectly to our preference. It melts in your mouth like butter. The vegetables are cooked soft, bathed in sauce, sitting on top of my rice. The broccoli is my favorite out of the vegetables. I scoot the mushrooms to the side of my plate when I hear a laugh from Ethan. He sticks his fork into one of them, proceeding to eat the fungus off of my plate.

"My hero," I say sarcastically.

"I have got to get you to experience more of this world."

"Absolutely, just not mushrooms," I tell him with a smile.

We eat and talk and laugh. We order some kind of fried ice cream for dessert, I'm not sure if it's authentic Japanese, but it's pretty tasty. I dip my finger into the chocolate and boop it onto Ethan's nose. He returns the gesture by smearing his chocolate-covered finger across my neck. As I laugh and grab my napkin to wipe it off, he snatches my wrist.

"Wait…" He leans in, not caring that we are in the middle of a crowded restaurant, and swipes his tongue through the chocolate on my neck. I freeze, unsure of how to respond as he licks all of the chocolate off, even sucking on my pulse point for a hot second. My heart picks up its pace. When he pulls away he laughs at my stunned expression.

"Waterfall. Now" is all I'm able to mumble as I drag him out of his seat, having already paid the bill.

Chapter 16

As we drive, I draw shapes with my finger on his palm. I tell him about the dress shopping fiasco and he tells me about the tours he did today. We laugh about what he did at the restaurant. When we get to Piku Ranch, I wait outside while he runs in to get the keys for the ATV. Ethan comes back out, turning on the head lights, driving us to our secret paradise. We hold hands, walking around on the sand, remembering our last time here. This is my favorite place in Kauai.

"Do you want to cross another item off my list?" I ask Ethan, mischievously.

He blushes, looking intrigued. "What did you have in mind?"

I walk toward the water, pulling down the straps of my romper. I turn around, shimmying it the rest of the way down my body, letting it pool at my feet. I kick it toward Ethan as he stands there watching.

"Are you going to stare at me or are you coming in?" I ask him, repeating his words from that first day. He gives a grin, unbuttoning his pants. I turn around, facing the water as I drop my panties, giving him what I hope is a sexy show. I slip my bra down my arms as I walk into the water, tossing it somewhere behind me.

"Skinny dipping, check." He comes splashing in the water behind me.

I swim out into the middle of the pool of water, directly

under the moonlight, circling around to face Ethan.

"*Maka nani*," he whispers.

"What does that mean?" I finally get the chance to ask.

"It means beautiful eyes. You have the most beautiful eyes I've ever looked into," he tells me.

Instead of saying anything, I wrap my arms around his neck, kissing him deeply.

"Come on," he says swimming into the cave.

When I swim through the waterfall, the cave is darker than before, with barely any light coming in from outside. If I couldn't feel him beside me, I wouldn't know Ethan was there. It takes a few seconds for my eyes to adjust to the dark and finally be able to see his black silhouette in front of me. I feel his calloused hands catch my waist.

"Zoey…" He wraps my legs around his waist, pressing me into the wall of the cave.

My body is ablaze with desire, it's a white-hot feeling. I need to feel him inside of me. I need to have him as close as possible, if not the water might carry him away. This primal urge is taking over my entire body. My fingers are pulling his hair, my calves pressed tightly into his back, pulling him into me. As he slides in, I feel the rubber resistance separating him from me. *How did he manage to get a condom out here?*

"Are you wearing a condom?" I ask.

"Yeah."

"Where did you get a condom from?" I ask, totally confused.

He laughs. "I had it in my hand. I swam out with it."

"Oh okay," I say continuing kissing him.

"Did you think I had a secret stash in my sex cave where I lure all my girls?" He laughs, reminding me of the conversation we had the first time we were in this cave.

167

"No, I didn't know you could use a condom underwater. I thought it would be just you and me this time." That seems to pause him, as he stops his movements.

"Is that an option?" he asks slowly with a raised eyebrow.

"I'm on the pill. I mean it's best to be safe with the condom, but I'm covered if we ever skip it."

"Jesus. Just the thought of that…" he trails off.

My orgasm hits hard. Clenching around him, as it courses through my body. I let out a loud scream that echoes through the darkness. His palms hit the side of the cave as he comes, thrusting up into me. I'm glad the water is supporting most of my weight or else we'd be drowning right now. He finishes with a shudder, pressing a kiss against my neck.

He swims backward, slipping out of me. I take a deep breath, submerging myself beneath the cool water. I swim through the waterfall, back into the middle of the moon's reflection, glimmering on the surface of the water. He follows behind me, seeing the used condom floating on the water out of his hand, he throws it onto the beach next to our clothes and joins me. I float on my back, completely bare to the universe above.

"You are the most gorgeous creature I have ever laid eyes on," he whispers to the stars.

We swim for a little while, embracing the sound of crickets and owls, absorbing all of the wonders nature has to offer us, before we head back to shore. As we dress, I slip my panties into my pocket, going commando for the rest of the evening. When he goes in to return the keys, I hang my panties on the parking brake. That should give the boys something to talk about when he finds them on his next shift.

"Ready to go?" he calls from the steps.

"Yes," I call back, jogging over to the Jeep.

Chapter 17

It's Sunday. I wake up alone in bed. Ethan has to take care of his dad for a while today, so he went home last night. We have the luau tonight but *what should I do until then?* Ethan told me I could come over and hang out at his place but I think I want some time to myself today. I think I'll go into town and get my nails done. I haven't done that since Mom took me last. It was our thing to go get our nails done once a month then we'd get lunch after. I slip into another romper, this one with a yellow floral pattern and my flip-flops. When my hair and makeup are done, I decide to slip out of my garden door to avoid any additions tagging along today. I walk into town in peace, finally having a chance to clear my head and process everything that has happened this week. Hopefully I don't have a mental breakdown in the salon.

I go to the small salon that I've passed several times this week. It's a pink building called Pampered in Paradise. They offer everything from manicures to massages. When I enter, I am greeted by the warm and welcoming smell of vanilla and cinnamon. I tell the receptionist that I would like the *mani/pedi* package. She tells me it will be about ten minutes and to have a seat. When I am taken back, I am surprised to be sat next to April.

"*Aloha*, darling!" she greets, excited to see me.

"*Aloha*, how are you?" I ask, happy to see a familiar face, one who I have no past with, at least not one that I can remember.

"I am good. Sundays are my days to get my nails done or go

out with the girls. Ethan takes care of Keone while I'm gone. Speaking of my son, why are you not with him right now? I thought you two were attached at the hip. I've barely seen him all week," she chuckles.

"Oh. I just needed some time for myself today. This week has been a lot."

"I bet, honey. You'd be crazy to act like everything is normal."

I breathe a sigh of relief from that. It's nice to hear that my feelings are validated.

"I wish my mom were here. Talking to her always helped calm my anxiety," I tell her sadly.

"I felt the same way about her. I know I can't take your mom's place but you're welcome to unleash your worries on me," she tells me wholesomely. "It's been a while since I've had a girl chat."

"Where do I start?" I exhale. "I didn't know what I was doing with my life before this trip. I didn't see a future for myself. I didn't apply to college, I barely graduated high school, I lost all of my friends. My aunt hates me for living with them and now that I'm eighteen, she will probably throw me out. I didn't have much money, but then I got that letter with $18,000, and I have no clue what to do with it. Ever since the accident, I've never seen myself being happy or having fun or finding love but this trip has changed all of that." I see her hide a smile at my mention of love.

"Ethan has been so wonderful but I feel like it's all a dream. Like at any moment, someone is going to come through with a needle and pop my happy little balloon. I feel like I shouldn't allow myself to be happy since my parents are dead. How can I be happy or do I even deserve to be happy?"

"Honey, you most certainly deserve to be happy. It's a sign of healing from your loss. You will never lose it, but the pain will ease. You will learn not to feel guilty about being happy. That's all they've ever wanted for you. The island has its ways of working magic on people, it holds its own healing powers."

There is a pause as I process what she's just said.

"Let me ask you this, do you want to go back to Michigan?"

"There is nothing for me there, all it does is bring back sad memories when I drive past our favorite ice cream place or walk through the flower section at the store. Every day I drive past the high school where I went and where Dad taught me to drive in the parking lot. I don't have a home there anymore." I close my eyes as the reality hits me. I can't go back to the life where I was barely surviving.

"You have a home here. With us. You could stay if you wanted. We have the spare bedroom that could be yours." She watches as I take in her words.

"You would let me move in with you?" I ask, completely raw and vulnerable. I've turned into a river of emotions.

"Of course. I've known you your whole life, even if you didn't know that I did. You have always been like a daughter."

"But what about Ethan? Doesn't it make me one of those obsessive, naïve girls if I move across the world for a boy I've only known for a week?"

"You wouldn't be moving across the world for a boy. You would be doing it for yourself. The boy is just an added benefit if that's what you want."

This is a lot to process, my anxiety levels running high.

"I am getting my hair done. Will you be in this area for a while?" she asks.

"Yes, I am getting a manicure after this."

"Would you like to get some lunch with me then?" She smiles.

"I would love that." A tear slips down my cheek.

"It's a date. I will see you in a little bit." She waddles away with the hair stylist, being cautious of her freshly painted toes.

"Hey! What color should I get? For Ethan?" I call.

She looks over her shoulder with a smile. "Orange."

I should have known. The nail tech grabs a bright orange polish with sparkles in it and I sit back watching her work.

*

I complete my manicure before April is done with her hair, so I wait in the lobby for her, sipping a complimentary cup of coffee. When she comes out, we walk a couple blocks to a deli-style restaurant. We each get a sandwich with homemade potato chips. It's a tasty lunch. My sandwich has turkey, bacon, cheese and some spicy mustard sauce on it. We talk about our separate lives as we dine. I tell her about my struggles since my parents died, how I secluded myself and gave up all hope. She tells me that it's okay, it's good that I can recognize it. I tell her things I haven't even told Ethan yet. She offers to help me move forward in whatever ventures I want to pursue. It lifts my mood to hear that someone is in my court, wanting to help me figure out my life. When we are finished with lunch, she asks what I am doing next.

"Well, we are going to a luau tonight but I still have a few hours, so I'm not sure what to do."

"Would you like to come home with me?"

"Do you think Ethan will be okay with that?"

"I'm sure he will be very happy to see you. Let's go," she says, walking away to her car.

When we get to their house, my heart is racing with the thought of surprising Ethan. I hope he's happy to see me, we weren't supposed to get together until later tonight. April opens the door, leading the way inside. All of a sudden, the bathroom door opens revealing a wet, shirtless Ethan with a towel wrapped around his waist. Water is dripping onto his chest from his hair, looking like one of those Hawaiian models from the racy calendars in the souvenir shops. I lick my lips involuntarily, admiring his tattoos.

"Hi, honey. How's it gone this morning?" April asks him, accustomed to seeing him fresh out of the shower, unlike myself.

"Dad is binge-watching the *Pirates* movies with Johnny Depp." His gaze flicks over to me. "What are you doing here?" he asks, surprised to see me standing behind his mom.

"Surprising you." I smile. He walks over, kissing me in front of his mom.

"Well, I am surprised."

"We ran into each other at the salon then got some lunch together," April informs him.

"Dear *Pele*. Hopefully, you didn't talk about me too much," he says, turning pink.

I look at April, knowing exactly what we talked about.

"Not at all, dear," she tells him. "I'm going to check on Dad," she says leaving us alone in the living room.

"Is everything okay?" Ethan asks me.

"Yeah. Everything is great," I reply happily. I pull him into an intense kiss, sliding my tongue between his lips to wrestle with his. I dominate this kiss, tugging his hair until I get the reaction I want, before stepping back.

He looks flustered, hair tousled and lips red. His cheeks are getting even brighter red.

173

"What was that for?"

"I really like you." He smiles as I tell him excitedly.

"I really like you, Zoey."

His mom walks out of the bedroom, pushing his father in his wheelchair.

"Woah you two! Get a room!" his dad yells covering his eyes. April smacks his arm.

"*Aloha*, Keone." I wave with a laugh, taking a step back from Ethan. He moves behind me, holding my hips firm. I'm wondering why he is so close when he presses his erection against my butt. Oh. I'm apparently being used as a human shield to hide his excitement from his parents.

"What are you doing here?" Keone asks me.

"I tagged along with April. Ethan is going with me and my family to a luau tonight."

"Good luck." He laughs.

"Yeah, hopefully it won't go so bad but who knows with my aunt. She'll probably complain about it being too Hawaiian."

April says something to Keone, drawing his attention, giving Ethan enough time to run to his room.

We make small talk until Ethan emerges from his room, grabbing my hand.

"We should get going," he says, dressed in a short-sleeved white button-down, black cargo shorts and his *slippahs*. He looks fantastic.

"Yeah, you're right, I still have to get ready. It was nice to see you again. Thanks for lunch, April."

"I'm sure we will see more of you around here soon." His dad smiles.

April leaves the dishes she had started washing to give me a hug.

"Be careful tonight. If your aunt does anything, you just come here, all right?"

"Thank you," I tell her hugging her back. "Thanks for today."

"Always, my dear."

I'm all smiles as we head out to the Jeep.

"I like seeing you this happy," Ethan tells me, reversing from the driveway.

"I like being this happy," I say, kissing his knuckles.

When we get to my place, it's empty. They must have already left for the luau even though it doesn't start for another hour and a half. Ethan takes a spot on the couch, watching a local surf competition while I go to get ready. I'm glad I hung my dress in the closet so it could de-wrinkle. I slip it on over a strapless bra and pink thong, then touch up my makeup, adding some pink glittery eye shadow that matches perfectly with my dress. I curl my hair, giving it volume and waves like a Pantene commercial, and swipe on some pink lip stick before it's time to meet my match. I strap the heels onto my feet, groaning that I am about to attempt to walk in them, especially in front of Ethan. Walking out into the living room, I do my best to avoid a baby giraffe impersonation. I watch as Ethan's jaw drops when he sees me.

"Woah," he gasps, hitting the off button on the TV remote, dropping it on the couch.

"Do I look okay?" I ask, feeling awkward being all dolled up like this. The last time I was this dressed up, was my sophomore homecoming dance.

"You look… you're wearing heels." His face is as red as if he got sunburnt, and his eyes wander over my body, down to my shoes. I can see the naughty thoughts, racing through his mind, are torturing him, as he tries to keep his composure.

"I know I just did my lipstick but will you please ruin it?"

Without another word, Ethan is pressed against me, arms clutching tight around my waist, devouring my mouth in a kiss hotter than the sun. This kiss should be illegal, with his teeth colliding against mine, his tongue deep in my mouth. He grabs my ass in both of his hands, rubbing me against his front, moaning into the kiss, and does it again. God, I wish we didn't have someplace to be right now.

I am the first to break for air. "We need to get going," I tell him, stealing a glance at the clock on the stove.

"Are you sure? I could give you a show right here," he smirks.

"Yes, it's already been paid for. But after, I'm all yours," I say swiping my thumb over his lips, wiping away the pink smears.

Chapter 18

When we arrive, Ethan pulls a pink tie out of his bag in the back seat. It's brand new, still in its store wrapper. He slips it over his head while I admire him.

"You got a tie to match my dress?" I ask, touched by his gesture.

"Of course, I had to match you. We will be the hottest couple in there and make your family look like donkeys." He smiles.

"Thank you." He grabs my hand as we exit the Jeep and walk to the entrance, where I spot my uncle standing there waiting on us. He glances at us as we approach.

"There you are. I was wondering if you would show. Everybody already went in but I have your tickets so I waited out here for you guys," he tells us, shaking hands with Ethan.

"Thanks," I tell him.

"Yeah, thank you for inviting me, sir," Ethan says politely.

"I'm glad you're here for her. Hopefully, my wife will behave tonight. You look lovely by the way," he addresses me at the end.

"Thank you."

"Tickets?" the guy at the checkpoint asks nicely when it is our turn in line.

My uncle pulls the printed tickets out of his pocket, letting the employee scan the barcode.

"There you are. Enjoy the show." He smiles, handing the papers back.

When we walk in, there are Hawaiian ladies in colorful *sarongs* handing out beverages. One has alcoholic drinks and the other has dressed-up, virgin beverages. I take two from the nonalcoholic tray, handing one to Ethan. There is a pretty flower floating on the top.

"I'll leave you guys to walk around," my uncle says, leaving us alone. There is so much to take in. The stage where the dance happens, the fire pit where they roast the pig, and a beautiful ocean view with the most amazing sunset lighting up the sky. Ethan and I walk hand-in-hand around the venue, admiring every detail. We stop at a woman who is giving hula lessons. I laugh, stepping forward to participate, craving the full experience of a luau, no matter how touristy it seems. Ethan stands away, watching me, as this is nothing new to him. I dance along to the five-minute hula lesson laughing and feeling bubbly. When it's over, I turn around to find Ethan standing there, with a pink hibiscus he picked off of the bush behind him. Standing in front of him, he places the flower behind my left ear.

"If you place the flower on the right side, it means you are single, but if you wear it on the left it means you are taken," he tells me sweetly.

I pull him over to the edge of the water, taking a picture of us in front of the sunset. This picture is going to be my new wallpaper on my phone. We continue walking over to the roasting pit that I learn is called an *imu*, watching as the men unbury the pig from the ground. The men are shirtless, only wearing *sarongs* around their waists, both of them covered in sweat and ash. The smell of pork wafting through the air is mouthwatering. Ethan explains the entire ritual as the men use shovels to dig up the pig. They cook the pig in the ground, on top of a bed of river rocks, using banana leaves which help in the steaming process. It cooks all day, entombed under leaves and burlap sacks, covered in dirt to keep all of the heat in. It's called kalua pork. A large dude, in a blue *sarong* with black hair tied into a bun on the top of his head, blows a giant conch shell, signaling the five-minute countdown until the dinner buffet opens.

"It's almost time," Ethan tells me, signaling that we should find our seats.

"All right," I say, letting him lead me away. We walk until we find my family's table, where everyone is seated already. On one side of the table sits my uncle, aunt, and Denise. The other side has Samson on the end beside two empty seats. I take the seat beside Sam and Ethan sits next to me, holding my hand under the table. The server swings by to grab our drink order. I quickly scan over the beverage menu noticing that they can make all drinks without alcohol.

"I'll have a virgin hula girl," I tell her. As soon as the words are out of my mouth, I realize what I just said. Everyone's eyes shoot to me in amusement and Ethan chokes on a laugh.

"That's not what I meant. Can I please have a non-alcoholic hula girl?" I ask, then hang my head.

Sam spits some water out of his mouth laughing. The server looks at me trying to keep her composure.

"Two of those beverages please," Ethan speaks for me, squeezing my hand. The server giggles, hurrying away. Ethan kisses my temple.

"Already making a fool of yourself this evening, I see," my aunt quips, rolling her eyes at me.

"That dress looks amazing on you. I told you it would. Did you like the heels, Ethan? I made her get them," Denise chirps cheerfully, trying to recover the mood after my aunt's remark.

"Don't be silly, dear. That dress is much more suited to your body, but it is quite revealing. My daughter wouldn't wear something so skimpy," Susan tells Denise, clearly not paying attention to what Denise wears on a regular basis. I see Denise look away to the stage. If only Aunt Susan knew about Denise's past of sleeping with the entire football team. The server brings back two pink drinks with flowers floating on the top. They look so elegant. I almost don't want to drink it.

"Two virgin hula girls." She giggles. I turn red and set my head on the table.

"Thank you," I mumble, leaving my head down until she disappears.

They announce that the buffet is now open and that we may serve ourselves. When our table gets up, I feel a quick pinch on my butt cheek, glancing back at Ethan, who is smiling. I grab his hand, leading him to the food. I pick a small portion of everything, including a small dish of *poi,* which I am surprised to find out Ethan does not like, even with it being a Hawaiian staple. I grab a purple roll, some of the roasted pig, a side of glazed carrots, a small side salad, grilled pineapple, filling my plate. I am excited to try everything, it all smells so good.

When we sit back down, I test out the *poi* first. Ethan watches as my face reacts.

"It tastes like wet dust," I grimace.

"I know. It's gross." He laughs, popping some pineapple into his mouth. He suggests that I try the *haupia* next, which is like a coconut pudding. It's light and tropical tasting, with the lingering aftertaste of coconut.

"Well, I see you're not hiding anything," Aunt Susan remarks as she returns to the table with just a small salad in her hands. We all look around to see who she is talking to when I notice her eyes on my plate.

"What does that mean?" I ask.

"It means you must feel comfortable that Ethan's not going to leave you after watching you pig out. Look at all of that food."

I look around at everyone else's plate noting they all look similar to mine. Piled high with bits of everything. "I got the same amount as everyone else," I defend.

"Well, if I were you, I would be watching what I eat, since you're dating someone so far out of your league, but it's your body, make it as big as you like." I can feel Ethan's grip on my thigh tighten as he fights back his anger.

I have lost my appetite but Ethan is watching me. Denise shoots me an apologetic glance. I try to enjoy my food, but it's not the same now. I take small bites, just enough to keep Ethan from saying anything. The rest of the meal is silent, all of us hoping to not hear anything more from my aunt. The server brings around a plate of desserts, full of cookies and pastries. My eyes light up as I glance at Ethan. The sweets look so artistic and crafted to perfection. I am the first to reach out and snag a cookie off the plate.

Susan smacks my hand, knocking the cookie onto the table. I look at her, paralyzed.

"That's it. I'm doing you a favor. Save some for the rest of us."

Ethan releases his hold on my thigh, standing up. He throws his napkin on the table, grabs my hand and helps me up.

"That's it. We're leaving," Ethan says hotly, as tears spill down my cheeks.

"What? She doesn't need to eat any more. I am trying to help you have a skinny girlfriend."

Ethan slams his hands on the table, making all the water

181

glasses shake, getting face to face with Aunt Susan, "I don't want a skinny girlfriend. I want one who's not afraid to put food on her fucking plate."

We squeeze behind Samson, trying to maneuver the tight seating arrangement. As we turn to head away from the table, my uncle stops us.

"Wait, Ethan," my uncle calls, standing up, digging his fist into his pocket. For a second, I think he's mad at us for causing a scene until I see him pull out the rental car keys.

"Yes, sir?" Ethan asks confidently, not having any issue with my uncle, but still standing ready to defend me from any more of this abuse.

"Can you give me a ride back to the house? I'm done here too."

Ethan and I both stare at him in shock but Ethan gives a quick nod of his head.

"What? You're leaving?" Aunt Susan shrieks at him.

Uncle Dan sets the rental car keys down on the table.

"Here, enjoy your luau," he tells her.

"Can I come too?" Samson asks quietly, avoiding his mother's eye contact.

"Of course," I tell him, giving him a small smile.

The four of us look at Denise who is glancing back and forth between us and her mom.

"Sammie! You too?" Aunt Susan wails.

"Yeah, Mom, you can't talk to Zoey like that. Not anymore," he tells her, defiance in his tone.

"Fine then. Denise and I will enjoy the show and desserts all to ourselves, isn't that right, baby?" She looks at Denise.

Denise sits there frozen, so the four of us start to walk toward the exit.

"Wait for me!" she yells.

"WHAT?" Aunt Susan screams loudly, slamming her hands on the table, disturbing the other patrons of the luau. Everyone is now staring in our direction.

"I like Zoey. She lets me tag along when she goes shopping and makes me breakfast. You're so mean to her and called her a slut. I'm the one who slept with the entire high school football team before junior year," Denise huffs, sliding out from behind Susan's chair.

"She is not a part of our family," she yells.

"Well, she's a part of mine and I'm not going to let you talk to her that way," Ethan finishes, signaling for us all to leave. When we reach the gate to the parking lot, our server runs up to us, hands full of reusable bags.

"Here, I overheard the argument at your table so we packed up some food for all of you. I'm sorry you didn't get to enjoy the luau. There are extra desserts and banana bread in this bag," she says handing us the bags.

More tears run down my face, as I step forward to hug this kind stranger.

"Thank you so much," I tell her.

"You look beautiful the way you are. Please don't listen to her."

My uncle has his wallet out, holding out a hundred-dollar bill to the server.

"Sir, that's not necessary. Gratuity is included in your ticket price."

"You deserve it. Please take it. We appreciate the food and are sorry for the disruption we have caused."

"Well, thank you, sir," she tells him politely, pocketing the money.

We exit through the gate, and head straight to the neon orange Jeep. Uncle Dan, Denise, and Samson climb in the backseat, sitting snug together. Ethan opens my door for me, offering me his hand for help stepping up. Ethan drives us back to the beach house in silence, everyone lost in their own thoughts. He never lets go of my hand, the entire drive. When we pull into the driveway, the five of us head into the kitchen, opening all of the bags to look through the food.

There is a large container of the kalua pork, some potatoes, a box of rolls, carrots, a little bowl of *poi*, a bowl of coconut pudding, and a container of salad. Plenty of food to feed five people. In the other bag were five miniature loaves of banana bread and a package of the desserts with enough to feed about ten people. At the bottom of the bag were five tickets to attend another luau at any date. That is so kind of them; I will definitely be emailing them a thank you.

I am hungry but I also don't feel comfortable enough to eat in front of people right now. I wonder if anyone can notice. None of us got to finish our meals.

My uncle gets plates out of the cabinet, handing me a plate, passing one to the others as well.

"No one here is going to say shit about what you eat, Zoey. Please eat," he tells me apologetically.

I set my plate down and hug him. He wraps his arms around me giving me a squeeze. I step back and everyone is looking at me.

"Thank you all for standing up for me. You don't know how much it means to me."

Denise and Samson hug me together. I do have a family after all.

I turn to Ethan who is smiling at me. I wrap my arms around

him, getting lost in his warmth and security.

"Come on, let's eat," Ethan states.

We all fill our plates with food and sit at the dinner table together. Denise hits a power switch, changing radio stations until some soft Hawaiian reggae music fills the air from the in-home audio system. Sam spreads the desserts on a platter from the cabinet and sets them in the middle of the table along with the banana bread.

"Now all we need is a virgin hula girl." Sam laughs. I toss my roll at him.

As we eat, Ethan speaks up, "If no one has plans for tomorrow, I can arrange an outing for all of us. Susan can't come, though." An awkward chuckle goes around the table. My uncle responds.

"That sounds like a great idea. Thank you, Ethan."

"Absolutely." I give Ethan a smile that lets him know that he didn't have to do that but I appreciate him.

We talk as we eat, sharing thoughts about the food. My uncle agrees that we need to reach out to the luau place and let them know how amazing the server was. It feels like Thanksgiving. Everyone is being nice and friendly. We chat and share stories and rate each dessert as we try them. The night has definitely had a turn of events but for the better. When we are done eating, my uncle is the first to dismiss himself.

"Ethan, I appreciate what you did tonight, son. You're welcome to stay the night, as long as it's all right with Zoey." He offers his hand to Ethan. Ethan stands up to shake Uncle Dan's hand with a firm grasp.

"Thank you, sir."

Uncle Dan grabs the whiskey bottle before he disappears down the hall, shutting the bedroom door behind him.

I smile at him as Ethan sits back down. I lean in, kissing his lips, forgetting we are in front of my cousins until Denise clears her throat.

"I'd prefer it if you didn't fuck on the dinner table. Please and thank you," she smirks.

"God, Denise," Samson says, running his hand over his face.

"I'd prefer to just hold you in my arms all night if that's all right," Ethan tells me, staring into my eyes, as if it were just the two of us.

I smile, nodding my head against his shoulder.

"*Aww*, aren't you two sweet," Denise coos, clearly jealous.

"I am going to go call Aiden," Sam says walking out on the back patio, leaving the three of us at the table.

"I think I will settle into a *Twilight* marathon on Netflix. You two have a good night." She winks heading off to her room. You would never take her as a Team Edward type of girl.

Ethan and I walk into my bedroom, closing the door behind us. Now that we are away from everyone, the thoughts are sinking into my head and I'm feeling deflated. Maybe my aunt is right, maybe I am too fat for someone like Ethan.

"Hey, you all right?" Ethan asks, pulling me into his chest.

"Yeah, I'm just tired," I lie, turning away. I reach behind me, struggling with the zipper of this dress. It's jammed in the fabric.

"Here, let me help." Ethan comes up behind me, taking the zipper out of my fingers. With gentle ease, he pulls the zipper down, as I clutch at the front of the dress, holding it against my chest.

"Can I wear one of your shirts?" I ask looking at the ground. He reaches into his bag and pulls out a plain white t-shirt. He doesn't let go of the shirt as I tug at it, trying to free it from his grasp.

"Zoey…" he whispers, looking saddened.

"What?" I ask as tears well in my eyes. I hate that he can see right through me.

"Drop the dress," he speaks.

Two tears slip down my cheeks. "No."

He steps closer to me, gently placing his hands on my arms. "Please let go of the dress."

As I hear the crack in his voice I let go of my grip on the dress, letting it fall in a circle at my feet. I sob as he pulls me against his chest, transferring all of the pent-up pain into teardrops, staining his shirt. He smooths his hand over the back of my head, letting me cry it all out. I mumble an apology for crying on him but he shushes me, letting me know he is here.

"Baby…" Ethan says gently as my crying slows.

"Yeah?" I whisper, feeling empty.

Ethan steps away from me, staying at arm's length. His face leans in as he places a kiss on my damp cheek. His lips move to my shoulder, then my bicep, down to my wrist. He lowers himself to his knees in front of me, placing a light kiss on the top of each breast, then moves to my stomach, where he kisses a circle around my belly button. He kisses my hips and thighs, even lifting my calf, kissing it, then the top of my foot. He pushes against my leg, telling me to turn around. When I do, he puts a kiss in the center of each butt cheek. He kisses all over my back as he rises, placing one last kiss on the back of my neck.

"What was that for?" I ask.

"You are the most beautiful girl I have ever laid my eyes on," he whispers, wiping the tears from my cheeks with his thumbs.

"There are prettier, skinnier girls," I say, looking down.

Ethan snags my chin with his fingers, pulling it back up so

that I look at him.

"Not in this universe," he says, gazing into my eyes, so close to my face that I can smell the guava from the cookie he ate, moments ago.

I can't resist kissing him. Once again, he has become my knight in shining armor, my protector, my everything. I wrap my arms around his neck, clinging to him with all of my strength. He matches my passion, his strong arms circling my waist, picking me up off of the floor. As I am becoming numb from the kiss, he pulls away, still holding me.

"I meant what I said. Let me just hold you tonight," Ethan says.

"Okay. Thank you, Ethan. For everything," I say as he carries me to the bed, pulling back the covers, setting me gently on the sheets. I slip his shirt on, removing my bra from underneath. When Ethan has slipped into a tank top and shorts, he slides in beside me, pulling my body into his arms.

"It's nice having everyone know that I'm here, but I hate wearing clothes to bed now. I've become addicted to holding your bare body against mine," he says into my hair.

Even my toes blush at his words. I feel the same way though. His skin is so warm, it's like having a personal heater to keep me cozy. The fabric between us blocks that warm intimacy.

"It is nice not having to sneak around," I respond, snuggling closer.

"Goodnight, my *maka nani*," he whispers.

"Goodnight."

Chapter 19

I am startled awake by a loud, metal clanging coming from outside of my bedroom. I swear this vacation has had louder mornings than back in Michigan. I look at the clock on the nightstand, reading that it's only seven a.m. Ethan is sitting up beside me, having been awoken too. Another loud crash has us out of bed and running into the kitchen, where we find my aunt throwing around pots and pans, yelling at my uncle.

"How could you let him stay the night?" my aunt shrieks.

Denise and Samson walk into the room at the same time as us, rubbing sleep from their eyes.

"What is going on?" Denise yawns.

My aunt notices Ethan and I standing there, now directing her anger toward us.

"That whore had her boyfriend stay over last night, and your father allowed it."

"Yeah, we know. We were here," Denise says as if it's old news and would like to go back to sleep.

"I don't want that kind of behavior flaunted around my kids. You are good kids, and I won't let her corrupt you. When we get back to Michigan, I want that skank out of my house." She points her finger at me, threateningly.

"Well, then, this will make things easier," my uncle says, pulling open the drawer on the counter, taking out one of those yellow legal envelopes. He slaps it down on the counter, in front of my aunt.

"What is this?" she huffs, snatching the envelope.

I watch as she pulls out a stack of white papers, the blood draining from her face, as she reads the cover.

"You've filed for divorce?" she screams, smoke whistling out of her ears.

"The kids are all grown up, and now that Zoey has finally turned eighteen, I thought it would be a good time. I am tired of your drama. You have mistreated Zoey, and blamed her for ruining our family, when it has been you this whole time. I am done watching you treat her this way. She is a member of my family and I hope she can forgive me for not saying something sooner." He gives me a sad side glance.

"So, you're going to leave your family, just like that?"

"No. The kids are old enough to make their own decisions. I am not leaving them, just you."

The room is silent as we all exchange glances. My cousins look like they are in shock.

"Zoey, here. This one is for you. I hope it helps repair things between us," my uncle says, handing me a smaller legal envelope.

"There is nothing to repair," I say giving him a nod, turning my attention to my envelope. Everyone in the room is waiting in anticipation as I open it, even Aunt Susan. My jaw drops as I read the document inside.

"This house belongs to me?" I ask, having to remind myself to breathe. I look around the room in disbelief.

"It was your parents. They always planned to return here one day. I transferred the title to your name. I figured you would like a place to call home. There's more," he says, handing me an ordinary, white, mailing envelope addressed from a bank. When I open it, there is a debit card attached to a bank statement.

"I have been renting this house through a travel company for the past three years. I put the money into a savings account. For you. So, you could have a fresh start. It's what your parents would have wanted." I look down at the paper noting the balance in the account to be over $600,000. I am tranquilized, every emotion washing over me like a rogue wave.

"Get out," I say staring at the documents in my hands. When I look up, everyone is watching me, unsure if they heard correctly. My cousins seem conflicted that I would be kicking them out, after starting a new friendship with them. I speak up to clarify.

"Susan."

"What?" she scoffs at me.

"Get. Out. If this is my house, I have the right to remove you from my property."

"You can't kick me out," she states boldly.

I hold up the title. "According to this, I can. Ethan's uncle is a member of the sheriff's department, I'm sure he could come and explain things to you."

"I have his number right here," Ethan says, holding up his phone with Charlie's contact info displayed.

Susan throws her hands up in the air, "So, you are kicking out your family from a vacation they paid for?"

"No. No one else has to leave. Just you. The rest of us are going canoeing." I smile at the other members of my family, happy to be starting fresh with everyone.

"Denise? Sammy? Please say that little bitch is lying," she begs, holding her arms out toward them, hoping they'll crawl back to her.

"We are staying with Zoey," Sam tells her, moving to stand closer on my side.

With one last scream, she stalks down the hall to pack her suitcase. An audible exhale passes around the group. Ethan rubs my shoulders and kisses the back of my head. We all head to our rooms to get ready, aside from my uncle who is already dressed. He stays behind to pick up all of the pans that are scattered across the kitchen. As I walk into my bedroom, Ethan grabs my waist, using my body to close the door behind me. He presses his mouth against mine, roughly, clinking his teeth against mine. My core instantly becomes liquid.

"That was so hot, seeing you stand up to her. Did you see her face when you told her to get out of your house?" Ethan says full of adrenaline-fueled desire.

I'm turned on from all the adrenaline rushing through my body. I didn't know I had something like that in me. I know we have to get moving but maybe we can take just a minute. I close my mouth over his, trying to convey exactly what I need right now.

"What about your family?" Ethan whispers.

"I don't care. This is my house," I repeat the words that feel so foreign in my mouth. My house. That'll take some getting used to. I am full of adrenaline-driven hormones that aren't going to stop until I have my way with the sexy man in front of me. Sliding my shorts off quickly, he covers himself with a condom, then picks me up, pressing me into the door.

"Fuck me, Ethan," I say lining myself up with his hardened member. He sheaths himself inside of me, letting out a groan. We don't have the time for foreplay so I'm not as wet as I could be, but the friction is an indescribable feeling, that has me turning into a slip-n-slide. We stay quiet as Ethan fucks me against the door; the only sound is his breath against my neck. I claw at his back, my insides squeezing around him.

He groans, slipping his hand between us, circling my clit with his thumb. I come undone around him, fireworks filling my vision. I cling onto him, receiving his last few pumps as I orgasm around his cock.

He pulls back, giving me a deep, satisfied kiss. He eyes the clock on the nightstand.

"Three minutes. That's a new record." He laughs. He pulls out, setting me on my feet. I lean my head against the door in an endorphin-filled, hazy state. Amazing orgasms, sweet revenge, and a beach house in Hawaii is enough to make anyone relax. For once in my life, I don't feel like I have to be a submissive angel with no voice. I can do what I want, say what I want. I have a power unlike ever before. This phoenix is ready to spread her wings and rise from the ashes.

"I'm not done with you, but for now we have a canoe trip to get to," I say with a new-found confidence, walking away to get dressed. I look sexually flustered in the mirror, my hair a frizzy mess, and my neck and lips bright red from the sweet torture of his mouth. Ethan stayed up last night after I fell asleep, looking into outings we could do with my family today. I am looking forward to a family adventure, without my aunt. I get dressed in this purple tank top that highlights my skin tone and some black shorts. I can't be looking too good, since I will be getting sweaty, and wet, later but I also don't want to look bad. I walk out of the bathroom to find Ethan in a black tank top, that shows off his muscular arms and tribal tattoos.

"You're staring at me the way you did on the first day we met." He grins.

Feeling bold, I tell him straight up, "I'm thinking the same thing I did that day. You look like you were made out of the volcanic eruption that built this island. Shaped by the hands of a

Hawaiian God."

He looks down at his clothes, face turning a deep red through his bronze skin.

"You are so sexy and I have no clue what you're doing with me, but I must be doing something right since you're still here." I chuckle to hide my insecurities.

"The way you look at me is the way that I see you," he says, sincerely.

I lean in to kiss him, but hear my aunt exiting the living room. Oh, this should be good.

Walking out of the bedroom, Ethan and I are the last ones to join the rest. My aunt is slamming her luggage through the house, banging it into the walls, screaming and crying.

"Where am I supposed to go?" she cries.

"I've already changed your flight, so you can head home today," my uncle tells her.

"I can't believe you are doing this," she smacks my uncle across his chest. He grabs her wrist to prevent her from striking him again.

"Hit me again and the only place you will be going is behind bars," he tells her through his teeth.

"I want to go home then," she screams, throwing a tantrum like a sleep-deprived toddler.

"Okay. I've already called for an Uber to come pick you up. He is waiting in the driveway," Uncle Dan tells her.

Susan huffs as she walks to the door. "I hope you are happy," she hisses at me.

"I am actually," I say, snuggling into Ethan's side, with a confident grin plastered on my face. She walks out, slamming the door behind her.

Uncle Dan turns to my cousins. "I am sorry this came so

abruptly kids."

"I kind of saw it coming," Sam says. "You and Mom haven't been happy in a long time."

Denise surprises us all, "I think it will be better this way. But what are we going to do when we get home?"

"Well, hopefully, she doesn't destroy the house. I suppose I will move out and find a new place for myself. You kids can stay with whoever you like when you're not at school."

"Thanks, Daddy," Denise says, hugging him. Her expression changes and she tenses, "What about Zoey?" She looks toward me, wandering where I'll go when we get back to Michigan.

"I'm not going back," I speak. As soon as I had the house title in my hand, I knew my decision.

"What?" Sam asks, surprised.

"I'm not going back. There is nothing for me in Michigan. You guys will go back to school. Uncle Dan has Susan and the divorce to deal with. I'm going to stay here. Try to find myself."

The room goes quiet. Everyone taking in my root-uplifting decision. I look to Ethan, hoping his reaction is a happy one. He seems like he's in shock.

"You're staying?" he asks.

"Yeah," I say, decided, staring deep into his eyes. He rushes over to me, wrapping me in his arms, spinning me in a circle. I rub my face against his chest, inhaling his scent. He backs away with a huge grin on his face.

"*Um*, is everyone ready to head to the canoe livery? Our reservation is in an hour," Ethan asks.

"Yes!" I say excitedly. Today is off to a great start and it's not even noon yet.

Chapter 20

We drive separately, Uncle Dan, Denise and Sam in their rental car and me alone with Ethan. It's only a quick drive to the canoe livery, but Ethan starts up the conversation that I'm not sure I'm quite ready to have yet.

"So, how are you doing?"

"I'm good. The weather is beautiful today," I say. The sun is bright in the morning sky, beaming over the natural landscape. The few clouds that are present, are white and fluffy, no raindrops in sight.

"Zo, you know what I mean. You have been on Kauai for eight days and A LOT has changed."

It's uncomfortable, trying to keep my composure. It is a lot, I know that. I guess I have been trying to stay numb to it all. A lot of choices have been put into my lap, when before this trip I had no options, no opportunities. The biggest decision I'd have to make was whether to wear blue or black jeans with my diner shirt. Now I have money, I have a home, I have a family. I don't know how to react.

"If I am being honest, I don't know how I am. I have never had so many choices to choose from before. I don't know what the right decisions are or who I need to please."

"The only person you need to please is, yourself," he says, giving my hand a squeeze.

All of a sudden, reality hits me. I am moving to Kauai away from the only state I've ever known. I am going to have to make really big decisions and fast. *What am I going to do for a living? Should I go to college? What about all of my stuff back home?* It's not much but I would at least like my dad's Bronco. *Oh shit! What if Susan trashes all of my stuff? Would she even allow me to get my stuff?* I am going to have to call work and quit, with no notice. They thought I would be returning this Friday. *How am I supposed to move to Kauai, not knowing anyone but Ethan?* I don't want to be the clingy girlfriend. *Can I be this wild and unscripted like my parents?* Before I know it, we are parked at the canoe livery, and I am in the midst of a full-blown anxiety attack, in the front seat of Ethan's Jeep.

"Zoey, Zoey! What's wrong?" Ethan says, panic setting into him. He's never seen me like this, no one has. I am gasping for breath, unable to get air into my lungs. My door jerks open, I look over to see Denise standing there, with Uncle Dan beside her and Sam behind him.

"What's going on?" Denise squeaks in fear.

Uncle Dan pushes his way in front of Denise, grabbing my purse off the floorboards.

"She's having an anxiety attack. She needs her medicine," Uncle Dan tells the group, plopping my bag onto my lap, and digging through it to find my pills. When his hand clutches around the bottle, he pulls it out, popping off the cap.

"Here, take one," he says, placing the white tablet in my hand. I look into his eyes, wondering how he knew about my anxiety.

"I've got water in the cooler," Ethan says, jumping out, to open the back. He returns with an ice-cold, glass bottle of water. I toss the pill to the back of my throat, swallowing it with a few gulps of water. I close my eyes, leaning my head back against the seat, taking deep breaths to slow my breathing.

197

"How did you know?" I pant, opening my eyes to look at my uncle.

"I've caught on over the years. I see you take one when you're really stressed, or when Susan would say something to you. You seclude yourself in your room when it happens. I haven't seen you take one since we landed here though."

"I haven't. Not since..." I nod my head toward Ethan, knowing he is the reason the attacks have stopped. I'm not brave enough to make eye contact with him. He has just seen a side of me that I was hoping to keep hidden.

"What set it off?" Uncle Dan asks.

I exhale, I have no strength to make up a story. "I am very overwhelmed by everything. Up until this week, I didn't see a future for myself. I didn't know where my life was heading. Now I have been handed more opportunities and possibilities than I know what to do with. Within the matter of seconds, I decided to uproot the only life I knew, to move to an island in the middle of the Pacific."

"You don't have to make these decisions all at once. You can take as long as you need. The only thing that is permanent, is death, so you do whatever you want until you find the best fit for you."

"I'm sorry. It all just came crashing down on me," I whisper.

"Hey, it's going to be okay. You have all of us supporting you." Denise touches my shoulder.

"Thanks. I think I'm okay now. Let's go get our canoe," I say, moving to get out of the Jeep.

My family walks toward the dock, my uncle grabbing the cooler out of the back, carrying it for Ethan. Ethan snags my hand, keeping me back.

"Hey, are you okay?" he questions, unsure of how to

approach the topic.

"Yeah, I'm sorry about that"

"It's all right. I was scared. I didn't know how to help you. We still have a lot to learn about each other. I'm sorry if I was part of the problem. If there is any way that I can help you, please tell me," he says, looking into my eyes.

"Hey. It's okay. I should have told you about my anxiety, but this week, I hadn't felt it, so I kind of thought it had gone away," I tell him honestly.

"I get it. It's a lot. Is there anything I can do for you right now?" He catches my wandering eyes.

"Kiss me," I tell him.

He obliges my request, stepping forward, taking my cheeks between his palms. His mouth is warm and inviting. This kiss isn't the normal, sexually fueled, kind; it's sweet and compassionate and lets me know he'll keep me safe. It's a short kiss, but he pulls me against his chest, giving me an embrace that soothes my worries. I exhale, releasing all of the built-up tension, feeling at peace in his arms.

With that, we walk in the direction of my family, who is currently waiting for us by the canoes.

Chapter 21

We get two canoes, meaning three of us have to ride in one. Denise jumps in with me and Ethan, against our playful protests, while Uncle Dan and Sam take the other. Uncle Dan pays for all of us. You can clearly tell which of us has been canoeing before. Denise got her flip-flop stuck in the mud on the riverbank and Ethan had to fish it out for her. I'm beginning to think that girl is a magnet to mud.

I have experience canoeing with my parents before, in Lake Erie. When I would be out of school in the summer, we would go camping, canoeing, and hiking, as long as it was within the state of Michigan so I could still work and volunteer. As soon as we are in our canoes, floating down the river, my body eases into a familiar rhythm. This river might help me do some self-reflection. We paddle slowly, enjoying our new serenity until Cardi B's "WAP" is blasting through the air. It makes me jump, turning around, I find Denise with a waterproof speaker.

"Let's get this party started!" she says raising her arms in the air like the spoiled princess, I know her to be.

"Oh my God! You're ridiculous!" I say, unable to contain my laughter. I stand up in the front of the canoe, giving her a little twerk as she slaps my butt. The boys are shaking their heads at us crazy ladies as we dance, somehow managing to keep our balance and not capsize our vessel. I drag my fingers through the water, feeling the coolness glide between them. The water is clear, making it possible to see small fish below the surface. I smack my hand against the surface, splashing Sam in the face. He wasn't expecting it, but I also wasn't expecting him to retaliate. The five of us splash around, Uncle Dan using the paddle to drench Denise.

After about an hour, we pull off to a side bank, where we get a drink and a snack, stretching our legs. The sun has managed to dry most of us aside from our butts. It's warmer today; the temperature in the high 80s, but at least there is a slight breeze. I walk into the water barefoot, feeling the cool liquid rush past my ankles. I stay barefoot as we canoe to our next stop, being able to dip my freshly painted, orange toes in the water.

Our next break is a riverside burger joint where we grab lunch. I order another pineapple burger, those becoming one of my favorites on the island. I split a basket of fries with Ethan, staring at him as I steal his fry from between of his fingers. I smile, kissing his cheek. This is such an amazing feeling, to be wanted and appreciated. I don't know why I freaked out earlier. There is nothing much waiting for me if I return to Michigan. Same boring job, same place my parents died, same house full of hatred for me. But here, Kauai is a fresh start, this is where my parents lived, I can adventure with Ethan, learning to live my life. I have enough money to cover me for a while. Maybe I'll look into the local college for the spring semester. Or maybe I'll take some time to travel. I'd like to see what the other islands have to offer. I am all smiles with the internal decisions I am making.

"Sup, Ethan? Zoey!" A familiar voice approaches us.

"*Howzit*, Jeremy?" Ethan exchanges a fist bump with his coworker.

"Getting a *loco moco*. Canoeing solo today. Who's all these *haoles* you got with you?"

"This is Zoey's uncle, and her cousins, Sam and Denise."

"Nice to meet you guys. Especially nice to meet you, honey girl." He winks at Denise.

That's all it takes to reel Denise in. "Hey there," she flirts, twirling her hair around her finger.

"Oh God." I look over at Ethan, watching his reaction to the train wreck that is about to happen.

"Who are you riding with, beautiful?" Jeremy asks Denise.

"Those two," she grunts at us as if we're disgusting.

"Well, there is room in my canoe, if you want to jump aboard."

"Yes, please," she answers in a trance.

My uncle is shaking his head as he finishes his milkshake.

"Ok guys, let's get back on the water," I say, not wanting to watch any more of whatever is happening between Jeremy and Denise.

"Good idea," says Ethan.

Instead of getting in our canoe, Denise rides with Jeremy, drool dribbling from the corner of her mouth.

We joke as the current carries us downstream, splashing each other with our paddles some more. Another water war gets started, but this time Uncle Dan and Sam are soaked. They ask to pull over so we do at a small sand bar so that they can wring out their shirts. Samson cleans his glasses, while Ethan and I tip their canoe over in the sand, to empty the excess water. Denise and Jeremy are standing under a palm tree, falling all over each other. I walk over to Ethan, wrapping my arms around him from behind, placing my hands on his chest.

"You're so warm," I tell him, rubbing my cheek against his bare back. He took his shirt off a while ago.

He strokes my arms with his hands, both of us basking in the rays of the sun.

"Hey, Ethan?" I ask.

"Yeah?"

"Thank you for everything," I speak.

"You're welcome." He spins around in my arms, catching me in a hug.

As I walk over to climb back into the canoe, my foot slips on an algae-covered rock in the water, bringing me to my knees. I feel a slight sting, but I brush it off thinking it's nothing until I see the red spirals in the water. I don't want to alert everyone that I'm injured, and ruin the day but as more blood pours from my knee, I know I need to fix it fast.

"Denise?" I whisper-shout, hoping she'll come over to me without putting up a fight and draw attention. "Denise?"

"*Uh*, what do you want, Zoey? Can't you see that I am busy?" she huffs, stomping over to me, taking her away from the man she fell in love with a whole ten minutes ago.

"Shit! That's a lot of blood," she gasps, kneeling beside me, as I clutch my hand over the gash. So much for not causing a scene. Ethan hears her easily and responds like an EMT.

"What happened?" he asks.

"I slipped on a rock. Cut my knee on something in the water. It's nothing," I reply, unaware of how bad the injury is.

"Here. Stand up," he says holding my hips to keep my balance.

When I stand up, I see it. The stinging I felt in my knee was a cut from a broken beer bottle that was buried in the gravel of the sand bar. Blood is oozing out of the profound cut, running into the river. It takes more than a little blood to turn my stomach, but I can see the look on Denise's face. She looks ready to hurl.

"Back up, Denise. Don't make yourself sick," I tell her, hoping to prevent her from vomiting.

"I have a first aid kit," Jeremy yells, jumping in his canoe to grab his bag.

"This is why I go to all the beach clean-ups *bruddah*. Tourists always be disrespecting our island. No offense to you all. You don't seem like the littering type. But some people don't get that this is our home," he says, pulling out a small box, containing gauze, bandages, ointment, blood clot powder, a hydration drink, and a survival straw. I watch as he and Ethan tear apart the contents, getting everything that they need to stop the bleeding. Ethan with a handful of gauze, clamps it over the opening, applying pressure. I cringe with the feeling, letting out a small wail. I see Jeremy rip the top of the clotting mixture open, eyeing me cautiously. Something tells me that this is going to hurt.

"Do it," I tell him, wanting to get this over with.

"Damn man. You got a scraper." He laughs. Pushing Ethan's shoulder.

Ethan pulls the gauze away, letting Jeremy dump the powder into the wound. I grab the side of the canoe, my body involuntarily lifting off the ground.

"Fuck." I scream, biting my tongue until I taste the metallic flavor of blood. Ethan places fresh gauze over the cut, wrapping it with an ace bandage. Once it is bandaged tightly, I attempt to stand on my own. Ethan, supporting me again. I can't put much pressure on my leg, but the pain is minimal at the moment due to the adrenaline rush.

"How does it feel?" Sam asks.

"Oh, amazing. You should try it," I respond sarcastically.

"Damn," Jeremy says with a smirk, letting me know he's impressed.

"Come on guys. I need to get Zoey to my mom, she'll fix her

up." Ethan takes command of the group. Great, I've ruined the family trip. He helps me sit, making sure to not get the gauze wet. I sit there helpless as he pushes the canoe back into the current.

"I hate this. I absolutely hate this," I pout, crossing my arms over my chest.

"It's going to be okay. We'll get you fixed up. Then you can resume being miss independent." Ethan smiles, catching on to my frustration. When we get back to the canoe rental building, Denise helps me limp over to a palm tree while we wait for the boys to return the canoes.

"So, Jeremy asked me out for dinner tonight," she squeals, excited.

"He's a cool guy, just your type." I laugh.

"Yeah, hopefully I won't get ditched in a parking lot on this date," she remarks insecurely.

"You won't. I've hung out with him. He's really nice," I tell her reassuringly.

At that moment, Ethan and Jeremy walk over to us, carrying Jeremy's personal canoe.

"What are you ladies talking about?" Jeremy asks.

"Girl stuff," I say innocently.

"Oh, sure. Girl stuff like this?" he asks, reaching into his bag for something. He pulls out my thong that I left in Ethan's ATV. I completely forgot about that. Ethan looks confused and Denise is straight up jealous that he's got another girl's underwear. I snatch it out of his hand, crumpling it up and stuffing it into my pocket.

"Was that?" Ethan starts to ask.

"Next time you leave your panties in your boyfriend's ATV, make sure he works the next day. The battery in mine died so I had to borrow Ethan's for a tour. What a surprise it was to find your butt floss on the stick shift. The better question is, what are you and Ethan doing at Piku after hours?" Jeremy's cackles fill the air. I glance at Ethan knowing damn well my face is red.

"Oh, my god! I caught them in bed together at our beach house!" Denise squeals, smacking Jeremy's arm playfully. "You two are freaks!" she giggles, eyeballing us up and down.

Ethan looks like he is enjoying every minute of this embarrassing charade. I, on the other hand, begin limping in the direction of his Jeep, making one of the slowest escapes possible. I can hear their laughter behind me. Ethan and Jeremy load his canoe on top of his car, and then Ethan joins me at the Jeep. We wave to Uncle Dan, Sam, and Denise as they leave in their vehicle. Denise, I know is about to spend the next few hours getting ready for her date. With the little upper body strength I have, I pull myself up into the Jeep, avoiding bending my knee. Also avoiding eye contact with Ethan. He pops up in the driver's seat, starting the engine. He sits there staring at me with a cocky grin.

"So... you left your panties in my ATV?" He chuckles.

Oh, God, here we go. "I was trying to be sexy. I didn't think about you having the next day off," I groan.

"Oh, it's definitely sexy. I just wish I was the one who found them." He laughs, pulling out of the parking lot.

When we get to Ethan's house, his parents' car is gone. He seems worried until we get inside. On the kitchen counter is a note from his mom explaining that she took his dad on an overnight trip to Oahu, since he had an early doctor's appointment there in the morning.

"Well, fuck," he says, raking his fingers through his hair.

"What?" I ask, watching him read the note in his hand.

"Mom and Dad went to Oahu for the night. I was going to have her take care of your knee. I guess we'll have to go to the hospital."

"Absolutely not." I rush out, putting up my defenses. I refuse

206

to go to the hospital unless it's a life-or-death situation. The last time I was in a hospital was to identify my parent's bodies after their crash. I can still remember the smell of the morgue, bleach and formaldehyde, so strong that it made my head spin.

"Zoey, we have to take care of your knee," he says, seriously.

"We can take care of it ourselves. We both have first aid experience and I was studying to go to med school so I know a little bit. I am sure we can bandage a minor laceration."

"You were planning to go to med school?" he asks, stirring the conversation for more details.

"Yeah, that was the plan. I dreamed of going to Harvard," I tell him, jumping up on the island of the kitchen, pulling up my bad leg. Ethan goes to the bathroom to get some basic medical supplies: tweezers, ointment, gauze, peroxide, bandages. I use a pair of scissors to cut off the current wrap. I slowly remove the gauze pad covering the wound, in case it starts to bleed again. It looks worse than I thought. It's a jagged cut, splayed open with some pebbles and dirt jammed in it from the river. You can also see a sliver of glass sticking out of it. That's going to be fun to remove.

"Wait… before we start." Ethan grabs a bottle of Terramana tequila out of the cabinet.

"Do you want a shot to help with the pain?" he asks, handing me the bottle.

"Good idea," I say, taking a long swing.

With some liquid courage in my veins, I use the tweezers to pluck the glass shard, about an inch and a half long, out of my knee. Blood starts trickling out, so Ethan applies some pressure with a towel. He places another towel under my knee, to catch the blood running out of the wound. We run some water over it, finding little relief from the coolness of it. My heart races with the thought of pouring the peroxide on.

"Hey. Look at me," Ethan says smoothly.

He leans in, capturing my mouth with his. It's a distraction as I feel him pour the peroxide into the wound. I bite down on his lip, to quiet my scream, as pain flares up my body. I break the kiss to gasp for air as the burning subsides into a throb. I am breathing heavily as he pats it dry, then using a Q-tip, he applies some antibiotic ointment to prevent infection. Finally, it's over, time to bandage it up. I put a piece of gauze first to absorb any extra discharge, then a large band-aid that covers my kneecap. Honestly, it could probably use a few stitches, but I'll work with what we have. When I am done, I relax back onto the chilly countertop, catching my breath. From the corner of my eye, I notice Ethan dabbing his lip with a napkin.

"Oh, my God. I'm so sorry!" I panic as I realize his lip is bleeding from me biting it while he poured the peroxide.

"No worries. I'm okay," he says, pulling the napkin away to show me that it is just a tiny slit in the middle of his lip.

"I'm sorry I bit you so hard," I tell him, rubbing his shoulder, asking for forgiveness.

"Don't be. I apparently liked it," he says, as confusion fills my face, he nods toward his crotch where an erection is clearly visible.

"Oh. You're kinky," I joke.

"I didn't know I was. Guess we'll have to experiment," he chuckles, clearing the counter of the discarded bandage wrappers, and used gauze.

"Thank you for taking care of me," I whisper, pulling him into a hug. I rest my head on his shoulder, finally being almost a foot taller than him in my current position on the counter. I yawn as the tequila is absorbed into my bloodstream, numbing the pain.

"Let's take a nap, you need to rest, then we'll go out. Does that sound okay?" Ethan offers.

"*Mhmm.*" I nod, sleepily against his chest.

Chapter 22

When I wake up, I am alone in Ethan's bed. According to the clock, I have taken a two-hour nap. My knee is stiff with a slight stabbing pain as I sit up, having slept off the buzz from earlier. His room is small, with blue walls. There is a hand-built bookshelf to my left and a TV mounted above a dresser to my right. He has a small nightstand with a lamp on it, representing the University of Hawaii's football team logo. There is a drawer I am curious to look in but choose to respect his privacy. There are plaques and medals hanging on his wall, from his high school soccer days. He was apparently a soccer star and captain of his team. There are also a couple of surf trophies. As I am spinning a medal between my fingers, the door opens.

"Oh. Awesome, you're awake. Are you hungry?" Ethan asks cheerfully.

"Of course," I say, following him out of the room into the kitchen. I smell whatever it is as soon as I step into the hallway.

"Wow. It smells amazing," I say, noticing he has set the table for two, having lit a candle in the center of the table.

"Thanks. I made *shoyu* chicken. It's chicken breasts soaked in a soy sauce marinade over a bed of rice," he shrugs.

"That sounds delicious. You didn't have to go through all this trouble for me." I smile, taking a seat at the table.

He brings the food over, sitting across from me.

"It's no problem. I already had it prepped in the fridge. I do most of the cooking in this house."

"I wonder why. Could it be because you are an amazing cook?" I see him blush.

"I wanted to be a chef, used to watch cooking shows as a *keiki* instead of cartoons. I wanted to go to culinary school, but that was before Dad's accident."

"You could still go," I tell him, chewing a mouthful of the rice.

"Yeah, I know. I guess I'm just afraid something bad will happen if I get my hopes up again." He tells me, showing me a glimpse of the innocent boy who lost his hopes and dreams all those years ago.

"What if something amazing comes from it though? You know, I know someone who is currently in the midst of life-altering decisions. She might be able to help you." I hint, implying myself.

"Oh yeah? Does she have pretty eyes?" he asks.

"She's told she does," I say, batting my eyelashes at him, making him laugh.

"So where do you want to go after dinner?" Ethan takes a bite, changing the topic.

"Honestly? I'm not feeling really good. You can probably just take me home, then go enjoy the rest of the day for yourself. I'm sorry. I want to go out but my leg and head are killing me," I say, sighing sadly into my bite of chicken.

"Let's stay here then. If you want to, I mean. My parents are gone until tomorrow. We can relax on the couch, watch movies, elevate your knee," he jokes.

"Such a romantic night. But yeah, if you don't mind. Are you sure you don't want the rest of the day to go run around?"

"Nope. I want to take care of my injured girlfriend."

"Girlfriend?" I ask, finally breaching this topic.

"Well, yeah. I thought that's what you were. If it's too soon, I understand," he says losing the light in his eyes.

I smile. "Okay then, boyfriend, what kind of movies do you like?"

"Oh no. I don't want to answer that. You'll laugh," he says, hiding his eyes.

"What?" I ask.

"Romance movies are my favorite." He blushes, stuffing his mouth with chicken.

"Seriously? You like romantic movies? Chick flicks?" I ask, shocked.

"Yes. I know, not very manly but I like the old-school love stories."

"What's your favorite?" I ask, full of desire and hope. Chick flicks are my favorite too.

"Well, anything Nicolas Sparks is always a good choice but my favorite is *Titanic*."

I smile looking away.

"Are you making fun of me?" he asks.

"Not at all. *Titanic* is my favorite too. And I love everything Nicolas Sparks. Or John Green."

"Yes. *The Fault in Our Stars* was perfect. Uh. I cried when Gus died," heh says getting animated about the movie. I watch his enthusiasm, falling deeper in love with the man in front of me.

"I've said too much." He rubs his hand over his face, embarrassed by his passion for romantic movies.

"No, keep going. I like it. Have you seen *50 Shades of Grey*?" I ask, quirking my eyebrow.

"No. I didn't feel comfortable watching it alone. Was it good?" His cheeks tint the lightest shade of pink.

211

"It makes you question sex stuff. Lots of asses and breasts too."

He looks like he is going to explode in embarrassment so he gets up to get a glass of water.

"Maybe we can watch it together sometime. Not tonight though. Tonight, is *Titanic*," I speak, watching him relax when I say that.

I try to clean up our plates but Ethan is quick to take them from me.

"I'll be okay," I tell him, avoiding the wince that wants to escape when I take a step.

"Go lay on the couch," he tells me. I walk over slowly sitting down while Ethan finishes up in the kitchen. When he comes in, he grabs the remote and inserts the *Titanic* DVD into the player. He grabs my leg gently, helping me lay back on the couch so that my knee is elevated. He climbs behind me, snuggling against my back with me in front of him.

"Is this, okay?" he asks, sounding unsure.

"Perfect," I reply.

We lay there in silence as the movie begins, completely content. I cannot remember the last time I just laid on the couch and watched a movie. I feel like this should be awkward with Ethan, but it isn't. It feels like we have been doing this our whole lives. Maybe this was something we did as kids. When it gets to the sex scene in the car, I feel him stiffen behind me and not just his chest. I scoot my butt back, rubbing against him with a smile.

"I'm sorry. They're in the car and it reminded me of having you in my car and I apologize. You're the first one I've had sex with in over a year," he says burying his face in the back of my neck.

"A year? Really?" I ask, surprised at that.

212

"Yeah, I shut down after Kaitlyn," he tells me.

I roll over, facing him. I stare into his eyes, taking him in.

"What made you pick me up on the Piku tour? I could've just sat in the car while the rest of them went."

"You were hypnotizing. Seeing you gawking at me on the beach then running into you the next day at the ranch? Something in the universe told me that it was fate, that I needed to get to know you.

"Do you realize how amazing you are?" I ask.

"What? I'm not," he replies.

"You have had so much thrown at you but you never give up. You find a positive in everything. You got a job to support your family when your dad was hurt. You cook and take care of him, rotating days to give your mom a break. You are an amazing man who is generous and sweet, even innocent in some ways."

"I am not innocent." He laughs.

"You can't keep a straight face when you tell me that you want to fuck me. You turn red and break eye contact, like you're saying a bad word and don't want to get in trouble." I watch his face heat up, as I call him out.

"You apologize for getting hard against me. The thought of watching *50 Shades* with me had you running for water. I'll even bet that you have never made love. That night on the beach was just as much your first as it was mine." He stares at me astounded.

"Who are you?" he whispers.

"What do you mean?" I question.

"How do you read me so clearly? You know me, unlike anyone else," he says, clearly taken aback.

"I don't know. I just feel this connection with you."

He looks at me in astonishment, then captures my lips with his. They are warm and inviting.

213

"Ethan," I moan against his mouth.

"*Hmm*," he sighs, moving his lips to my neck.

"I haven't showered and we got all sweaty and gross today. I'm not ready for you to see me all disgusting yet. I want to keep the illusion that I naturally smell like coconut."

He backs up with a laugh and smiles.

"Do you want to take a shower?" he asks, prepared to get it ready for me.

"Yes, please," I tell him, sitting up on the couch. He helps me limp into the bathroom, bringing me a fluffy blue towel that I am excited to wrap myself in. It feels so soft. He shows me how to work the shower and then closes the door as he leaves, giving me privacy to undress.

A twig falls out of my bra as I pull it over my head. Wonder how long that has been there. It feels good to strip these clothes off, I sweated more than I realized. I hope Ethan didn't smell me when we were lying together. As I step in the shower, my knee fully covered in the saran wrap that Ethan had insisted on, the water running over my body lulls my aches. It dawns on me that I have no other clothes to change into, I'll have to put my sweaty ones back on. Unless Ethan will let me borrow something. That's a cute thought, me wearing his clothes. I rinse my head, looking around at the shampoo bottles. I use the one Ethan had pointed out, letting me know it was his. It smells woodsy, like the forest, with a hint of cologne, just like Ethan. It's enough to put butterflies in my stomach. I wash my hair, scrubbing my scalp, feeling the slight sting of sunburn where my hair parts down the middle.

His body wash smells like the ocean, salty, crisp and clean. I squirt some on the wash cloth he gave me, rubbing circles over my body, washing away all of the dirt and sweat from the day. I do my best not to fall over while I bend down to wash my feet. When I am all clean, I rinse over my body one last time before shutting off the shower, stepping out. The towel is even better than I had imagined, like a soft bear hug. I dry my body and shake the towel through my hair. I wrap the towel around me, tucking it under my armpit. Ethan is walking out of his room, with a small stack of clothes in his hand, when he spots me and freezes. He approaches, holding out the clothes.

"I didn't know... I got some... if you wanted to..." he rambles, having lost his train of thought at my appearance in a towel. I smile.

"What was that?" I ask, teasing.

"I got you some clothes in case you didn't want to wear yours. But if you don't want them, that's fine, they will probably be a bit big on you anyways," he says, eyeing the floor.

Seeing his shyness at me in a towel has my heart leaping. It makes me want to get his reaction all the time. In a surge of confidence, I lift my arms, letting the towel fall to my feet. His eyes dart to me, dilated and unsure of how to proceed. I smile like the Cheshire cat, grabbing the t-shirt from the stack.

"Thank you," I say, doing my best to be seductive while pulling his shirt over my head. His eyes are wide as he stands there silently watching, as I grab the pair of shorts from him.

"I guess I'm the one going commando today," I hint at him, reminding him of my birthday. His face fills with fire, staring at me swimming in his clothes. They are big on me, but at least they are clean.

"You look... I like... nice," he stutters, realizing his mess up, rubbing his hand over his face.

"Were you going to shower too?" I ask.

"Yes. Yes, I am definitely showering," he says, rushing

toward the closet where the towels are kept.

"Hey, Ethan?" I call.

"Yeah?"

"Don't squeeze anything too hard in there." I wink, watching him disappear into the bathroom.

I go to the kitchen for a glass of water, feeling parched all of a sudden. *What do I do while he showers? Do I just sit back down on the couch?* I'm sure he wouldn't mind if I looked around. I look around at all of the family photos decorated around the rooms. Pictures of Ethan when he was a baby, at the beach, playing soccer. There's even one of him dressed like a little chef in an apron and top hat, rolling out what looks like cookie dough. It makes me miss my home; my parents had all of our photos hung up on the walls, in colorful frames. The house we lived in burned down shortly after their accident. The cause was never identified but I lost everything I had left of them. I browse over the bookshelves and stacks of DVDs, mentally choosing our next movie, *The Breakfast Club*. I walk back to Ethan's room, thinking I'll give him a little surprise when he comes in. I take his clothes off and lay back on his pillow, completely naked. I can't help but feel exposed by my pasty white body, the stretch marks on my stomach, and the thickness of my thighs. But for some reason, I don't think it bothers Ethan. Right as I am chickening out of this bold decision, the door opens, revealing Ethan with a white towel wrapped around his waist, water dripping down his torso. How does he look so sexual from something as simple as taking a shower?

"Fuck me." He stops in his tracks, eyes exploding from his head.

"That's actually what I had in mind," I say, biting my lip, not allowing myself to break the intense eye contact happening

216

between us. He stalks forward, pressing me back into the mattress, slowly straddling me, keeping his towel anchored around his hips. He kisses me thoroughly, igniting my core. I move my legs to wrap around his back but am stopped by the stabbing pain in my knee, causing me to flinch and break the kiss.

"Your knee. We can't do this right now," Ethan frowns.

"Like hell, we can't. I just can't bend my knee. It'll be fine as long as I keep it straight," I reassure him, pulling his head down to resume our kiss. I would really like to have my way with him right now. Especially since the release of endorphins would probably help with the pain.

"You are the first girl I've had naked in my bed," he whispers against my lips.

"Hopefully the last," I whisper, guiding him back to my mouth, losing myself in the taste of his minty toothpaste, having freshly brushed his teeth. I pull his hand between my thighs, letting him know what I want. I pull my right leg up, wrapping it around his hip, leaving my bad one down on the bed, doing my best to spread myself open for him. His fingers trace my folds, teasing my wet entrance. He slowly sinks one finger inside and I let out a breathy exhale, like this was what my body has been longing for, and its desires are finally being fulfilled.

"You're so wet," he whispers against my neck, sucking lightly. His words do nothing but increase my arousal.

"Ethan, please," I beg, unable to stand his teasing.

He grabs a condom from the mystery drawer on his nightstand, tossing the wrapper to the floor, sheathing himself in the thin latex.

"Ready?" he asks, looking for consent as per usual. It makes me love him even more.

"Yes." As soon as the word leaves my mouth, he is slipping

inside of me. A relief washes over me, as if this is home. I wrap my good leg tighter behind his back.

"Wait, can I change positions? It might be easier for you," he suggests.

"Okay," I reply, curious as to what he has in mind. '

He slips out of me, moving off to my side. He helps me roll over so that I am facing the wall, with my bad leg on the mattress. He wraps his arms around me, holding me against his bare chest, pulling my top leg back over his thigh. Just the thought of this new position has me tingling in excitement.

"Is this okay?" he asks.

"Yeah, I think so," I answer, still unsure of how this position is going to feel.

He slides into me from behind, guiding himself with his hand. He holds my hip as he thrusts in, setting a pace that builds my pleasure. This position feels so intimate and emotional, as he hugs me, kissing my neck, gently thrusting into me. Coming in from behind has him thrusting into my g-spot, causing me to scream out, and grab hold of his hand. He thrusts again into the same spot.

"Fuck!" I scream, overcome by pleasure.

"Oh, I must be doing this right if you're going to use language like that," he whispers sensually against my ear, causing me to squeeze around him. I hear him grunt, then repeat the action. It doesn't take very long until I'm on the brink of explosion. His fingernails are digging into the skin on my hip, his lips scorching my neck, biting my earlobe. I am overly sensitized when he thrusts again, pushing me over the edge. I squeeze his hand as I orgasm around him, keeping him thrusting into that spot.

"Fuck me!" I scream as the pleasure hits me in waves. I bite down on his pillow, letting him thrust hard and fast as he finishes, the pleasure too much to handle.

"Fuck, I'm coming," he pants, grinding into me one last time.

I lay there spent, trying to regain some composure. My entire body has turned to liquid, that orgasm being the most intense one I've ever felt.

"That was…" Ethan tries to get out but he is the same as me apparently; unable to form words.

After a few minutes of laying against my back, he pulls out, rolling over to dispose of the condom. I carefully roll over to meet him face-to-face in the middle of his bed.

"That was fucking fantastic. I could feel that orgasm in my toes," I tell him, with sleep-saturated excitement.

"It was almost unbearable how tightly you squeezed around me," he says, attempting to control his breathing.

"I couldn't hang on after you said 'fuck me.' That was really fucking sexy," he whispers, I can feel my body turn back on. I internally tell it that we are going to bed now.

"I'm so sleepy," I say, drowsily.

"It's okay. Get some sleep *maka nani*." He kisses my forehead.

Chapter 23

In the morning, Ethan drives me back to the beach house on his way to work. He traded his day off with Liam to take us canoeing yesterday. When we get there, he walks me into the kitchen. As we're saying goodbye beside the kitchen island, a loud crash comes from Denise's room. Both of us take off down the hall, throwing her door wide open, to find Denise in all her glory, riding Jeremy, who looks mortified when he catches sight of us walking in. They knocked a lamp off the bedside table. When she notices the door open, Denise stops her bouncing, looking over at us like we are interrupting her, completely unashamed of the situation. My uncle comes walking in behind us.

"What the hell broke?" he asks, walking into the doorway. He looks up finding his daughter in the middle of intercourse. Denise slides off Jeremy, pulling the blankets up to cover herself.

"Jesus Christ, Denise!" He covers his eyes, shaking his head, before backing out of the room, and heading into the kitchen. I look at Ethan and then back to the scene on the bed. I'm unable to hold my laughter any longer, clutching my sides it hurts so much. Ethan starts laughing with me, finding it to be pure gold that the tides have turned and he now has something to harass Jeremy with.

"Hey, man, we have to get to work," Ethan says, walking backward out of the room.

I smile at the two of them, Denise finally getting caught, not being the perfect daughter. I think back to the morning she walked in on me and Ethan, so I decide to have some fun.

"So, how was it?" I squeal the way she does, throwing my hands in the air.

"Ugh! Get out!" she yells, throwing a pillow in my direction.

I laugh as I exit, meeting my uncle, Ethan and Sam in the kitchen.

"I gotta go, babe. I'll see you later," Ethan says, pecking my lips lightly.

A few minutes pass as the three of us make small talk, until Denise walks out of her bedroom with an embarrassed Jeremy trailing behind her. She opens the garage door, practically throwing him out, without so much as a goodbye.

"Was that the guy from yesterday?" Sam asks while eating a bowl of cereal.

"Shut up, Sam," Denise huffs angrily, taking a seat at the kitchen island.

"You know, you should really lock the door if you're going to sneak a guy into your room," I sarcastically quote her words back to her with a big grin on my face.

"Fuck off," she whispers.

Uncle Dan just leans against the counter, sipping his cup of coffee, watching us interact.

"I have some emails I have to send today, so you guys are on your own," Uncle Dan tells us.

"Who do you have to email?" Sam asks.

"The lawyer and a realtor. I have to get things in motion because I don't know what to expect when we return home. The sooner I get things finalized, the better," he says.

"Oh, okay. Well, ladies, do you want to spend our last day in Hawaii at the beach?"

"I don't know. Can we walk there or do we have to ride

Jeremy?" I ask, making Uncle Dan spit out his mouthful of coffee. He puts his cup in the sink, walking away with a groan. Denise throws her toast at me.

"We are definitely walking," Sam says, uncomfortably.

We all separate into our own rooms to get dressed for a day at the beach.

Chapter 24

As the three of us are walking across the parking lot toward the beach, I hear something coming from a nearby vehicle. I look over to see a guy grabbing a girl's arm, trying to force her into the backseat of his car. The redhead is resisting and looks scared. Looking closer, I notice that it's actually Kaitlyn being grabbed by the man. I don't know what's going on but I'm not about to watch any girl be taken advantage of, even if she is my enemy. I start walking in their direction.

"Hey!" I shout, catching their attention. When both heads turn to look at me, I find it's Sergio, the douchebag Denise went out with. *Wonder how Kaitlyn knows our lovely friend here.*

I walk up to them, Sergio dropping his grip from Kaitlyn's arm. She takes a step back allowing me to step right in between them, chest to chest with a guy that's a foot taller than me.

"What's going on here?" I direct toward Sergio.

"Nothing, sweets, just trying to have a good time," he replies flirtatiously.

"It doesn't look like she wants to have a good time with you." I point my thumb at Kaitlyn behind me.

"She just doesn't know what I can do to her. I was trying to show her when you interrupted."

"I interrupted because it looked like you were trying to force a girl into your car to rape her. And after what you did to Denise, I have a hard time believing that your intentions are good."

"Listen here, bitch… " he says, slapping me across the face.

My vision blurs red as my body temperature rises, preparing to fight this guy.

"If I can't fuck with her, how about you get in my backseat. I'll teach your mouth how to act in the presence of a man." Both of his hands grip my breasts, squeezing hard.

Before my mind is caught up, my body is in kill mode. It feels like when the Winter Solider was activated. My right fist punches him in the gut while my left hand grabs the back of his hair, ramming my good knee straight up into his crouched-over face, breaking his nose. When he lands on his back on the pavement, I wait for the precise moment for his knee to fall to the side before stepping on his groin. He lets out a strangled cry, like an animal being run over by a car. When he is down for good, I turn to address Kaitlyn.

"Are you all right?" I ask.

"Yeah. Why did you come to my rescue?" she asks quietly, not meeting my eyes.

"You might hate me for being with Ethan, but I wouldn't have stood by while that creep raped you."

My cousins must have noticed I wasn't with them on the beach because Denise is running this way.

"Woah, what happened?" she asks, gesturing toward my face and the injured jerk on the ground.

"Sergio here was trying to get Kaitlyn in his car against her will. I stopped him before he could do anything serious. Can you call the cops, please? That fucker is going to jail," I tell her before taking a seat on the concrete parking block. Sam checks me out, making sure I'm not injured, before checking on Kaitlyn. Kaitlyn sits beside me as we wait for the police to show up. Sam stands over Sergio to make sure he doesn't try to run but I've got my eye on him. With that final blow I delivered to his balls, I would

224

be surprised if he can walk for a few days.

"You're kind of a bad bitch," Kaitlyn says, pushing herself into my shoulder.

"My dad made me take self-defense classes growing up," I say, explaining my skills.

"Well, it was worth it. Thanks for saving me," she says, sincerely.

"Anytime," I say, watching as the police pull in with their lights and sirens.

We stand up to speak with the cops, as they exit their police cruiser. I recognize Ethan's uncle.

"*Aloha*, we seem to be making this a habit," he says, giving me a smile.

"*Aloha*, Charlie. Thanks for coming."

"It's my job. So, what happened?"

I let Kaitlyn begin the story, then speak up when I come into the incident. I tell Charlie everything I saw and how Sergio grabbed my breasts, threatening me. They took pictures of Kaitlyn's arm which has started bruising by now. Charlie and the officer who was with him handcuff Sergio, before placing him in the backseat of their vehicle. He was groaning in pain the whole time. I told Charlie how I took him down in case it's relevant in court. Even Denise came forward and reported the other night, how Sergio tried to get with her before dumping her in a parking lot. Sam looked mortified, hearing about all of this for the first time. Up until now, we haven't spoken of that night.

"You're something else, Zoey," Charlie tells me. I'm not sure whether it's a compliment or insult, but with the smile on his face, I will take it as a good thing. "We will take his ass to jail and get all the paperwork filed. Here is my card, ladies. If you need anything else, don't hesitate to give me a call," Charlie says, handing the three of us a card. He hops in the police cruiser with his partner, driving Mr. Fuckface to jail. I secretly hope he does time for all the nastiness he has attempted. I do hope I don't have to go to court for anything though.

"Well, who's ready to get back to the beach?" I ask my family, hoping to return to the happy walking and talking we were doing an hour ago.

"Me!" Denise shouts, raising her hand.

We turn to leave, but I hang back to check on Kaitlyn.

"Are you sure you're all right?" I ask.

"I'll be okay. I'm going to head home, try to forget about all of this," she says.

"Okay. Put some ice on your arm. He's put away now, you have nothing to worry about," I tell her reassuringly.

"Yeah. Thanks again."

"No problem," I say, heading in the direction of my family.

"Hey, Zoey!" Kaitlyn calls.

"Yeah?" I say, turning back around.

"You're good for him." I don't have to ask to know whom she is talking about.

"Thanks," I tell her. I walk back to the beach, planning to spend the next few hours soaking up all that the sun has to offer.

The next five hours are spent snorkeling, sunbathing, and listening to Samson's spiel about the damage the sun can cause to the human retina. After Denise hit him with a face full of sand, he shut up. I am officially roasted and figure I'll need some more of that magic aloe gel tonight, but it's worth it. Having a day with my family like this has been amazing. It's something I never thought I could have.

"Well, it's our last night. What should we do for dinner?" my uncle asks when we return from the beach. We can all hear his stomach protesting.

"Pizza," Samson says.

"Steak," Denise chimes, of course.

"Pasta," I say.

"Okay, that was no help. I'll decide. Get in the car," Uncle Dan says lightheartedly, ushering us all out the door. Even he seems to be more at ease since Aunt Susan has left.

We end up at this authentic Hawaiian restaurant, ordering the family fish platter that turns out to be bigger than we all had imagined. There is shrimp on the sides of a plank of mahi-mahi filets, enough to feed seven people. It's ginormous, even coming with a family-sized tossed salad with a lychee dressing that was out of this world. If moving to Hawaii wasn't for a fresh start, it would definitely be for the food.

After dinner, we walk around the other restaurants and shops, Denise picking up a few more trinkets to take back home. I notice Sam pick up something, I know is for his boyfriend, even though he doesn't need it. It's an individual condom that says 'Ride the Big One.' Oh god. I take them to the gelato shop that Ethan took me to on our first date. Of course, Denise has complaints about the number of calories. I get the tiramisu flavor this time, remembering my first kiss, on the beach, under the moon, just a few days ago. Man, how things have changed. I am in need of a shower after dropping it down the front of me in the car ride. Uncle Dan could have warned me about the speed bump we encountered.

Stepping out of the shower, I am wrapped in a serenity. I brush my teeth, heading to bed. I am sunburnt and drained, ready for the cool sheets to embrace my body.

Chapter 25

I awaken to the sounds coming from the kitchen. I am beginning to think there is no such thing as sleeping in, here in Hawaii. I can hear Denise specifically. I get myself ready before heading out of my room. Everyone's luggage, except for mine, is in the kitchen. Denise is scurrying around, double-checking that she hasn't forgotten anything.

"Don't worry. If you forget something, I will mail it to you," I say, in an attempt to calm her.

She stops in her tracks. "That's right. You're staying." Her voice sounds almost sad. She scampers back into her bathroom before she lets herself show any sign of emotion. I decide to make breakfast for everyone while they finish packing. I whip up my signature eggs, that I know will please Denise, alongside some toast with guava jelly that I picked up from the local farmer's market. I even toss on the bacon that we all forgot about. I cook on the griddle outside, enjoying the sunrise over the water. I pour four cups of coffee, set up four plates full of food and yell in the house to let everyone know that it's ready.

When the four of us sit around the table, it's silent, peaceful, as if we are each taking a minute to ourselves. My uncle has a somber expression on his face, alerting me something is going through his mind. He is the first to speak.

"I have a lot to figure out when we get home," he says staring at his plate, stirring his eggs with his fork.

"We'll be there for you, Daddy," Denise states, nodding her

head.

"You two will be going back to school soon. Zoey is staying here. I have to find a new place to live and get all of the paperwork sorted out. I wonder what your mother has been doing since she got home?" he contemplates.

"Probably destroying my room," I say, taking on the somber expression myself now. Denise looks at me like she feels sorry for me, like she knows as well as I do that is highly likely, knowing Aunt Susan.

"I'll replace anything she destroys." My uncle looks at me.

"Thanks, but I think I have everything important here with me. I'd really just like my dad's Bronco one day," I begin wondering how I can get it over here, making a mental note to look into the shipping costs later.

"If any of you ever need anything, feel free to call. I can always book a flight there or if you need to get away from home, you all are welcome to come here," I tell them.

Sam speaks up. "How can you be so nice to us after the past three years of us being complete asses?" His question surprises me. I'm not entirely sure how to answer.

"Because she is just like her mom." My uncle smiles. It makes a tear well in my eye, being compared to my mom.

"What are you going to do here all by yourself?" Denise asks.

"I don't know yet. I'm thinking about visiting the other islands. I'll eventually look for a job. Maybe check out the local college. I might even go on a trip across the world." I'm exploding with happiness on the inside as I list my options. My world is now full of possibilities, ones I've never even dreamed of before; I don't know where to begin.

After we finish breakfast, I go help Denise finish packing. I actually have to sit on her suitcase while she zips it shut, thanks to her excessive swiping of Uncle Dan's credit card. When she is good to go, we load the car. Their flight leaves in two hours, but they still have to return the rental car. It's finally time to say goodbye.

Sam is the first to hug me. "Thank you for forgiving me. If you need anything, don't hesitate to ask."

"I will. Same to you. I hope all works out with Aiden." I see him smile at the mention of his boyfriend's name. My uncle is next.

"I hope you find a better life here, Zoey. I'm sorry I didn't do more for you in Michigan."

"I get it. All is forgiven. If you need a place to stay until things cool down with Aunt Susan, you can always come back here."

"Thanks. I may take you up on that," he says, giving me one last squeeze before he slides in behind the wheel, Sam already in the passenger seat, having called shotgun before Denise. It's like they are still twelve and thirteen.

"I'm sorry for being a bitch to you for so long. You are actually pretty cool. I'm glad we get a chance to start over," Denise begins.

"Me too."

She hugs me. For the first time, Denise actually hugs me. This is the start of something new and it feels good to finally be accepted into my family.

She loads into the backseat as I stand in the driveway, waving as they pull away. Once they are gone, I head back into the kitchen. I tidy up the breakfast dishes, placing them in the dishwasher, starting the cycle. I decide to start making this place mine. First, stripping all of the sheets off everyone's beds, placing them in piles beside the washer. My plan is to move into the master bedroom tonight. I will also need to go grocery shopping at some point but hopefully Ethan will go with me, so I can learn the best places to shop.

Upon entering the master suite, I make a note to buy new curtains, the current ones don't fit my vibe. I also want some colorful sheets. I grab a pen and paper, writing down everything I want for my bedroom. I write the grocery list on the backside of the paper, filling every line. I have a lot of shopping to do. When I open the bedside drawer, I find a pair of diamond earrings that belonged to my aunt. These were one of her favorite pairs. Guess they are mine now. There are a few cleaning supplies in the house, so I start in on the master bath. I scrub the toilet with the toilet brush, sweep and mop the floor, use a special environmentally friendly, grime cleaner in the outdoor shower, then sanitize the sink counter. I bring in my own bathroom supplies, filling the empty spaces. My makeup is now displayed on the sink, my shampoo and body wash are in the shower, my pink loofah is hanging from the hot water handle. I am excited to try out the outside shower tonight.

I have decided that I want to visit the other islands of Hawaii. I have the money to take some time off, and I think that's just what I need. I'll visit Oahu first, then Maui, staying as long as I want on each island. I have no set time frame. I want to gain some experiences and live adventurously, like my parents. This island has opened my eyes to how much the world has to offer. I'm hoping Ethan will come with me. My plan is to ask him when he gets here. Shit, it's already five o'clock. He is supposed to be here at five thirty p.m.! I finish putting the freshly washed sheets on the king-size bed in my new room and head to my old room to change. I'm going to surprise him with the orange lingerie I bought the other day. I quickly put some curls in my hair, applying a thick coat of mascara and red lipstick. The feathers on the bottom of the outfit tickle my thighs. I situate myself on the kitchen island in front of the door so I'm the first thing he sees when he walks in. It's five twenty-nine p.m.; he should be here any second. One minute later, exactly on time, there is a knock on the door.

"Come in," I yell from my current position.

The door opens, welcoming Ethan in a black dress shirt, carrying a bouquet of roses. I wasn't expecting him to surprise me. I was supposed to be the one surprising him.

"Woah," we say in unison. He's staring at my breasts the same way I'm staring at the shark tooth necklace hanging over his pectoral muscles.

"I thought I'd surprise you since it's your first night alone in your house," he says.

"And I thought I would surprise you since it's my first night in my house," I reply.

He walks over to the counter, setting the roses off to my side, and places his palms on my thighs.

"What did you have in mind for the night?" I ask, twirling his necklace between my fingers.

"Before I walked in that door, my plan was to take you to a nice dinner and watch the sunset on the beach."

"And now?" I ask seductively.

He looks up into my eyes. "Now I want to ravish you in every room of this house."

"That sounds nice. There's actually something I wanted to ask you."

"What's that?" he whispers against the skin of my neck, as he begins kissing down my throat.

"Do you want to go to Oahu with me?" I ask.

9 781804 399064